Coach Arlin gripped Jessica by the arms. "Listen to yourself. Do you have any idea how ridiculous you sound? We can't go over there and accuse that poor girl of faking an injury just so she could somehow sabotage your routine."

"But that's what happened!" Jessica insisted. Her eyes swelled with tears. She *knew* that Dawn Maven oiled the bar and made her fall. Why wouldn't anyone believe her?

"You have to put this meet behind you and concentrate on the next one," Coach Arlin told Jessica, handing her a tissue.

"Or concentrate on the California Games," Amy offered, patting Jessica on the back. "We're still going, you know."

Jessica nodded and forced a smile. She dried her eyes. "You guys are right," she said. "There are other things I should be concentrating on."

Namely *revenge*, she thought as she narrowed her eyes at Dawn.

Hang out with the coolest kids around!

THE UNICORN CLUB

Created by Francine Pascal

Jessica and Elizabeth Wakefield are just two of the terrific members of The Unicorn Club you've met in *Sweet Valley Twins* books. Now get to know some of their friends even better!

A sensational *Sweet Valley* series.

TEAM SWEET VALLEY

JESSICA GOES FOR THE GOLD

Written by
Thomas John Carmen

Created by
FRANCINE PASCAL

BANTAM BOOKS
NEW YORK · TORONTO · LONDON · SYDNEY · AUCKLAND

JESSICA GOES FOR THE GOLD
A BANTAM BOOK : 0 553 50503 3

Originally published in USA by Bantam Books

First publication in Great Britain

PRINTING HISTORY
Bantam edition published 1996

Conceived by Francine Pascal

Produced by Daniel Weiss Associates, Inc,
33 West 17th Street, New York, NY 10011

Cover photo by Oliver Hunter

Bantam Books are published by Transworld Publishers Ltd,
61–63 Uxbridge Road, Ealing, London W5 5SA,
in Australia by Transworld Publishers (Australia) Pty Ltd,
15–25 Helles Avenue, Moorebank, NSW 2170,
and in New Zealand by Transworld Publishers (NZ) Ltd,
3 William Pickering Drive, Albany, Auckland.

Printed and bound in Great Britain by
Cox & Wyman Ltd, Reading, Berkshire.

To Jeanne and Burt Rubin

Acknowledgment

The author wishes to acknowledge CRAG
Gymnastics for their help in the research for this book.

ONE

"Where's Amy Sutton?" Caroline Pearce asked, glancing around Mr. Bowman's classroom. Kids were slowly trickling in for the after-school meeting of the sixth-grade newspaper, *The Sweet Valley Sixers*.

Caroline leaned across the aisle toward Sarah Thomas. "I bet she's with Ken Matthews. Have you seen how chummy those two have gotten?"

Elizabeth Wakefield let out a sigh. She and Amy were co-editors of the newspaper. "Amy has gymnastics practice tonight!" she informed everyone before the rumor could get any juicier.

Caroline Pearce was the biggest gossip at Sweet Valley Middle School. Elizabeth usually ignored her, but when the gossiping was directed toward her best friend, Elizabeth had to speak up.

Caroline shrugged and tossed her long red hair

behind her shoulder. "Whatever you say, Elizabeth. You're the boss."

Elizabeth rolled her eyes. "Well, you're probably all wondering why I've called this special meeting of the *Sixers* and why I've asked Todd Wilkins and Aaron Dallas to help us out."

"I bet it has something to do with the upcoming California Games," Todd said, running a hand through his wavy brown hair.

Elizabeth grinned. Todd was her sort-of boyfriend. "You're absolutely right. The California Games are coming up in just a few weeks." Just thinking about the Games sent shivers up and down Elizabeth's arms.

The California Games were the middle school equivalent of state championships. But because of budget cuts, they were only held every other year.

"I don't know whether any of our teams will qualify for the Games," Elizabeth went on. "But I thought this was a good time to focus on *all* of our sports teams."

"That's great," Aaron Dallas said. "I'll do soccer. I bet the soccer team goes all the way to the California Games." Aaron was captain of the soccer team.

"I bet the volleyball team does too," Maria Slater said. "Right, Elizabeth?" Both Maria and Elizabeth played on the volleyball team.

"I don't know." Elizabeth scratched her chin. They certainly had a shot at going, but Elizabeth didn't want to get her hopes up just yet. "We've still got quite a few games ahead of us before we can say for sure," she said realistically. "But I wouldn't be surprised if the girls' gymnastics team goes."

"I heard they only need one more win!" Caroline spoke up.

"That's right." Elizabeth knew that this time Caroline's sources were correct. Elizabeth's twin sister, Jessica, was on the girls' gymnastics team. Some people might even say she *was* the girls gymnastics team. Her experience on the Boosters (the middle school cheerleading squad) and ballet lessons had really paid off for her.

Elizabeth herself was never all that excited about dance class. She even quit a while back. But Jessica loved it! And she had branched out to tumbling and gymnastics.

Though Elizabeth and Jessica were identical on the outside, with their long sun-streaked blond hair, blue-green eyes, and matching dimples in their left cheeks, they were completely different on the inside.

Besides gymnastics, Jessica was into clothes, parties, boys, and gossip. She belonged to an exclusive group of girls called the Unicorn Club, which was made up of girls who considered themselves to be the prettiest and most popular girls in the school. Most girls in Sweet Valley would have killed to belong to the Unicorn Club. Most girls—except for Elizabeth.

Elizabeth secretly referred to the Unicorns as the "Snob Squad." She was into more serious things like school, reading, and the *Sixers*. But despite all their differences, Jessica was still Elizabeth's favorite person in the world. And Elizabeth was proud of her sister's gymnastics accomplishments.

"I saw Jessica practicing on the uneven parallel bars the other day," Sarah spoke up. "She was on the high bar, and she did a handstand and then turned around on her hands."

"I think that's called a pirouette," Elizabeth said.

"Wow!" Sarah said, her brown eyes widening with awe. "Isn't that something they do in the Olympics?"

"Jessica probably does a lot of moves they do in the Olympics," Aaron said. "I'll bet she takes the gymnastics team all the way to the California Games."

"I'll bet she does too," Elizabeth agreed. "And *The Sweet Valley Sixers* will be there to see it happen!"

"There's Janet." Jessica Wakefield's best friend, Lila Fowler, pointed down the row of eighth-grade lockers. "Do you want to ask her or should I?"

"I'll do it," Jessica said boldly. Janet Howell may have been president of the Unicorn Club, but Jessica wasn't afraid of her. At least, not *too* afraid. "Hey, Janet!" she called as she and Lila made their way through the crowded hallway.

"Hi guys," Janet said, taking a book from the top shelf of her locker. "What's up?"

Jessica took a deep breath. "We, um, just wanted to let you know that, well, we're not going to be able to make the next few Unicorn Club meetings."

Janet stared at Jessica as though she'd said she was going to wear her blue striped blouse with her green plaid skirt. "What do you mean you're not going to be able to make the next few Unicorn Club meetings?" she demanded, hand on her hip.

"Well, you know Lila and I are on the gymnastics team." Jessica glanced at Lila, and Lila nodded her agreement.

Janet's eyes narrowed into tiny slits.

"And well, with the California Games coming up—"

Janet's face relaxed. "Hmm. I see."

"You do?" Jessica and Lila asked in unison.

"Of course, missing club meetings is not something to be taken lightly," Janet said in a warning tone. "But I suppose I have to consider the Unicorn image in the long term. And when you bring home the gold and silver medals from the California Games, you're going to make the Unicorns look really good!"

"Yeah, well, I'm only going to get the gold medal," Jessica pointed out. "They don't give the same person both a gold and a silver medal. At least, not in the same event."

Lila snorted. "She meant you'd bring home the gold and *I'd* bring home the silver," she said, rolling her eyes.

"Oh," Jessica said, rolling *her* eyes in response. Lila was good, but she wasn't good enough to get a medal. Jessica was the only one on the Sweet Valley team who was good enough to get a medal, and the whole school knew it. But if she said so out loud, Lila would only get mad, and Janet, who was Lila's first cousin, would take Lila's side. Then Janet might order Jessica to attend all Unicorn Club meetings.

Jessica couldn't worry about Unicorn Club meetings when she was supposed to be concentrating on winning a gold medal for her school. So, for the good of the school, Jessica kept her mouth shut.

*　　*　　*

"I'm sorry, Donald," Coach Ingram laid a sympathetic hand on Donald Zwerdling's shoulder.

Donald looked down. He'd tried out for the boys gymnastics team for the second time that season. With only a few weeks until the California Games, Adam Farber had moved away and Coach Ingram was desperate to replace him. But not, apparently, desperate enough to take Donald.

"Your floor exercise wasn't too bad," Coach Ingram told him.

Donald glanced up hopefully. "I'll bet you really liked my Donald Zwerdling Zzzpecial!"

Coach Ingram raised an eyebrow. "You mean that uh, handspring you did at the beginning? Your form was a little awkward, but basically it was OK. I really needed someone who's strong on rings, though," he said apologetically.

Donald sighed. He picked up his gym bag and headed for the door. But before he reached it, Tom McKay stepped in front of him.

"Hey Zwerdling!" he said with a sneer. "Maybe you should try out for the *girls'* gymnastics team!"

Bruce Patman snickered as he walked past.

"Very funny," Donald said as he stomped out of the gym and toward the lockers. His blue Sweet Valley jacket dragged along the floor. *Face it, Donald,* he said to himself as he spun the dial on his lock. *You're never going to be an athlete. You're never going to be popular.*

Donald stuffed his jacket into his locker and slammed the door closed. He had to face the facts: he was a disaster at every sport he tried. He couldn't pass or receive a football. He couldn't hit a baseball. He did make a basket once when they played basketball in phys ed, but he also whacked Coach Cassels in the head with the ball a couple of times. After that, Donald didn't have the nerve to try out for the basketball team.

Still, Donald thought as he walked down the hall, a guy had to be athletic somehow. And he'd been sure that gymnastics was *his* sport. If only it weren't for the stupid rings!

He stopped outside the girls' gym to tie his shoe. He glanced up and noticed Jessica Wakefield spinning around the uneven parallel bars, her blond ponytail trailing behind her. Everyone said Jessica was going to take the team to the California Games.

Donald stood up and watched her more closely. Her routine didn't look *that* hard. Except for when she went from the top bar to the bottom bar backwards, with her legs spread apart. That looked a little tricky.

Now she was back on the top bar. She brought her legs up and over and then somersaulted into a dismount.

"All right, Jessica!" Mary Wallace cheered.

Jessica smiled as she brushed a few loose strands of hair out of her face. Lila Fowler, Amy Sutton, and Mary Wallace crowded around to congratulate her.

Donald stepped into the gym and looked around. Uneven parallel bars. Floor. Vault. And balance beam. There were no rings in girls' gymnastics.

Donald took a few more steps into the gym. Tom had been teasing him, but was joining the girls' team such a bad idea?

*   *   *

As Jessica headed over to the vault, Lila grabbed her arm. "What's Donald Zwerdling doing here?" Lila asked. She said Donald's name as though it gave her a bad taste in her mouth.

"Beats me." Jessica shrugged. Donald was talking with Coach Arlin, but with the California Games so close, Jessica had much more to think about than what Donald was doing in their gym.

She turned to watch Amy Sutton, who was running hard toward the vault. But she wasn't running hard enough for a handspring vault. Jessica winced as Amy's hands hit the horse and her body careened to the left. *She's not going to make it,* Jessica thought.

Mary Wallace was there spotting her, but there wasn't much she could do. Both Amy and Mary went down with a thud onto the thick blue mats.

Jessica and Lila ran toward them. "Your run-up was too slow, Amy," Jessica said. Since she was the best gymnast on the team, she felt it was her duty to give constructive criticism.

"Why don't you watch me?" she asked as Amy untangled herself from Mary. "I'll show you how it's done."

She walked back to the end of the mats and raised her hands. Then she sprinted down the runway as fast as she could, feeling the wind through her hair. She hit the springboard just right, kicked her legs up over her head before her hands even hit the horse, and came down flat on her feet, without so much as a bobble.

"Very nice, Jessica," Coach Arlin called from

across the gym. Donald Zwerdling was still standing there with her.

"I can do that," Donald said with confidence.

"Yeah, right," Jessica snorted.

"No, really," Donald said with a smile that revealed his buck teeth. "I can." He started over to the vault. "If I do a vault just like Jessica's, will you let me on the team?" he asked Coach Arlin.

"Let you on the team!" Jessica shrieked.

"You can't join our team!" Lila cried.

Ms. Arlin ran her hand through her curly brown hair. "Donald, this is a *girls'* gymnastics team."

"I don't mind." He shrugged. "If you don't want to see my vault, let me show you what I can do on the floor. I've got this awesome move I call the 'Donald Zwerdling Zzzpecial—'"

"What's a Donald Zwerdling Special?" Amy Sutton asked.

Donald turned toward her. "Not 'Special.' 'Zzzpecial!' And uh, I can't really describe what it is. You have to see it to really appreciate it." He straightened his shoulders. "But I'll tell you this," he said, cocking his head as though he were trying to sound modest. "Coach Ingram was impressed."

"Then why aren't you on the boys' gymnastics team?" Lila asked. "What are you doing over here bugging us?"

"Uh, well . . ." Donald gave a nervous laugh. "Funny you should ask that."

Lila snorted. "Yeah, real funny," she said, tossing her sleek brown hair. "I bet you didn't make the boys' team, did you?"

Donald reddened. "Well, not exactly—"

"Ha! I knew it!" Lila exclaimed triumphantly.

"Yeah, but I would have," Donald said, sticking up his index finger. "If it wasn't for one *very* small detail."

"And what might that be?" Jessica asked sweetly. "Lack of talent?"

Donald cast his eyes downward. "Lack of expertise on the rings," he mumbled.

Jessica, Lila, and Mary burst out laughing.

Donald looked up. "But I swear I've got a killer floor routine! And I can get over the horse—"

"You have to do more than get over it," Amy pointed out.

Jessica grabbed Lila's arm. "Come on," she said. "Spot me on the bars. We don't have time for this."

"But it'll only take a minute!" Donald pleaded. He dropped to his knees and raised his folded hands in prayer. "Please?"

"I'm sorry, Donald," Coach Arlin said. "If this school didn't have a boys' gymnastics team, maybe I'd think about it."

Donald rose to his feet. He looked like he might cry. "Just let me show you what I've got," he begged.

Coach Arlin sighed. "It won't change my mind," she warned.

Donald's face brightened. "Sure it will. You'll see." He moved to the floor mats in the middle of the gym. "Step aside, girls," he said to Brooke Dennis and Melissa McCormick, who were practicing back walkovers on the mat.

Lila's mouth dropped open. "Coach Arlin!" she cried.

Coach Arlin spread her hands out helplessly in front of her. "We might as well humor him for a few minutes. It'll take less time than arguing with him," she explained.

Jessica sighed loudly as she watched Donald parade around the mat. He looked about as graceful as a duck on roller skates. He flung his arms around haphazardly as he leaped and twirled. Then he attempted what Jessica thought was supposed to be a cartwheel. He put his hands down and swung his body over to the side. His feet didn't even go as high as his knees.

"This is so stupid!" Lila said.

Donald turned. "Here comes my big move!" he said with a weak smile.

Jessica yawned. "I'm breathless with anticipation."

Donald took a running start, jumped about six inches into the air, and fell flat on his stomach.

Coach Arlin winced.

Lila and Mary Wallace giggled.

"Some big move!" Jessica said.

"I'm OK!" Donald said as he hopped to his feet. "Let me try it again."

He backed up to the corner of the mat and took another running start. This time when he leaped into the air, he came right back down onto his feet.

"How nice," Lila said with a smirk. "Donald can jump."

Donald grinned nervously. "One more time," he said, backing up to the corner of the mat again.

"Uh, I think we've seen enough," Coach Arlin interrupted. "We've got a big meet tomorrow, Donald."

Donald's face fell. "Well, maybe I could just hang around and practice with you guys?" he suggested.

"No way!" Lila cried.

"I don't think that's a good idea," Coach Arlin shook her head.

"But I won't be in the way," Donald cried. "I promise! I could even help out. You know, get clean towels. Refill the chalk tray. That kind of thing." His eyes sparkled with hope.

Jessica sighed. She almost felt sorry for him.

"I really want to make the gymnastics team," Donald begged. "And the only way I will is if I can hang around the gym and practice with the professionals."

"Well, I suppose we could use a towel boy around here," Coach Arlin admitted.

"What?" Jessica cried. She didn't feel *that* sorry for Donald.

"You've got to be kidding!" Lila moaned.

Coach Arlin shrugged. "With the California Games just around the corner, we can use all the help we can get!"

"Really?" Donald's whole face lit up. "Do you mean it? Oh, this is going to be so great. You won't regret this, Ms. Arlin. I promise you won't!"

Jessica groaned. She didn't know about Ms. Arlin, but *she* was regretting it already.

TWO

"Wow! Look at all the people!" Elizabeth glanced wide-eyed around the gym. It was Thursday afternoon and she was down on the floor with the Sweet Valley girls' gymnastics team, covering today's meet against Weston for the *Sixers.*

"Who on earth *wouldn't* be here?" Jessica asked. She was on the floor doing straddle stretches. "After all, we're as good as in at the California Games."

"Well, we still have to win one of the next three meets before we're in for sure," Amy remarked as she rolled her shoulders, warming up.

Jessica waved her hand like it was a sure thing. "No problem," she said. "We'll probably win all of—oh, great!"

Jessica stared at the gym door and Elizabeth followed her gaze.

"It's Donald Zwerdling," Amy murmured. "He really wasn't joking."

Donald was dressed in a red-and-black Sweet Valley Girls Gymnastics Team T-shirt and gray sweatpants that just barely covered his knees. He was carrying a huge stack of freshly washed towels.

"Hi Donald." Elizabeth waved.

"Shhh!" Jessica grabbed Elizabeth's leg. "Don't call him over here."

But it was too late. Donald sauntered over to them with a huge smile on his face. "Hello, team-mates. Are we all ready for the big meet?" he asked from behind his load of towels.

"We?" Jessica raised an eyebrow. "Just because Coach Arlin let you carry towels and stuff does *not* make you part of this team."

"Jessica!" Elizabeth hissed. Jessica had told her about Donald auditioning for the girls' gymnastics team. She could understand why her sister wasn't thrilled to have a boy hanging around the gym with them, but she couldn't help but feel sorry for Donald. It had to have been hard for him to be turned away from the boys' gymnastics team.

Donald shifted his load of towels. "Just because I'm not actually competing doesn't mean I'm not on the team," he said with a smile. "Coach Arlin even said I could be like an honorary member."

Suddenly his stack of towels toppled to the floor.

Jessica shook her head in disgust. "Even honorary members should have a *little bit* of coordination." Then she rose to her feet and walked away.

Poor Donald, Elizabeth thought.

But Jessica's comment didn't seem to faze him. "Wait!" he yelled, scrambling after her. "I've got a towel for you!"

"I'll get my own towel, thank you very much," she said over her shoulder.

Donald sighed as he dropped to the floor to re-fold the towels.

"Don't mind her," Elizabeth said, bending down to help him. "She's under a lot of pressure."

"I know." Donald nodded. "She's the one with all the classy moves. If she does well today, the team goes to the California Games. If she doesn't, well. . . then there's always Tuesday's meet."

"She'll do well," Elizabeth said with confidence. Jessica thrived under this kind of pressure.

Jessica took a deep breath as she slipped her fingers into her hand grips, preparing for her turn on the uneven parallel bars. She commanded herself not to be nervous. After all, performing on the bars was her favorite part of the competition, and she knew her routine perfectly. It was a killer routine too—full of complicated hand changes and death-defying leaps from one bar to the other.

"Knock 'em dead, Jessica," Mary Wallace said from the bench. "I know you'll get us into the California Games."

Jessica smiled as she clapped high fives with Mary. Then she approached the bars, her heart pounding with excitement.

She stepped up to the chalk tray, squirted her grips with water, then coated them with chalk. *This is it,* she told herself. She went to stand in front of the low bar, facing the two judges, and took a deep breath. She raised her arms, and when she got a nod from the head judge, she mounted the low bar.

If there was any noise in the gym, Jessica didn't hear it. Her body seemed to be on autopilot, flowing naturally from one move to the next. She did a perfect kip to handstand, then a glide kip, squat to a stand on the low bar. She leaped to the high bar, swung, then came back in a blind back-straddle over the low bar. She'd never felt so strong.

Then Jessica leaped to the high bar for her big move. She did a long hanging kip, then casted to a full handstand on top of the high bar and did a pirouette. The crowd went wild.

Jessica's heart raced as she performed her final steps: a turn, two giant swings, and her flyaway dismount. She landed cleanly, with no extra steps. Perfect!

"All right, Jessica!" Lila yelled.

"Way to go!" Coach Arlin applauded.

All around the gym, people were jumping up and down, cheering for her. Her face glowing with excitement, Jessica turned around and waved to her public.

Jessica's heart beat faster than ever as the judges tabulated their scores. Finally the head judge stood up. "Nine point seven," he announced.

"*Ahhhhh!*" Jessica screamed as she ran toward her teammates and threw herself into her coach's arms. She'd never gotten such a high score before! No one on their team had ever gotten such a high score!

And no one on the Weston team could possibly get a higher score, Jessica was sure of it. Which meant only one thing: Sweet Valley was going to the California Games!

Donald watched as Jessica Wakefield hugged everyone in sight. She was so psyched, it didn't look like she even knew *who* she was hugging. *Hey, maybe she'll even hug me!* he thought with a grin.

He grabbed a couple of towels and made his way through the crowds. "Step aside," he said. "Towel boy coming through."

"Don't you mean 'dough boy?'" Lila asked, poking him in the stomach.

Donald stepped around Lila and handed Jessica a towel. "You were pretty awesome out there, Jess. You don't mind if I call you Jess, do you?"

Jessica raised an eyebrow. "Are you kidding me?"

Donald cleared his throat. He figured it might be a good idea to change the subject. "Anyway, do you think you could teach me that routine?"

Jessica glanced at Lila and the two girls broke into giggles. Then they turned to leave.

Donald leaped forward and grabbed Jessica's arm. "Well, maybe you could teach me part of it?" he begged. "If I could just learn some of those moves, Coach Ingram would have to let me on the boys' gymnastics team. And if I was on the boys' team," he said with a pointed glance toward Lila, "I wouldn't be hanging around here bugging you!"

Lila put on a fake smile. "Believe me, Donald, I live for the day when you're out of my hair. But I doubt Coach Ingram would be interested in what you can do on the uneven parallel bars. Boys compete on the horizontal bar and on the parallel bars. They don't compete on uneven parallel bars."

Donald hit his forehead with the heel of his hand. "Just like girls don't compete on rings or the pommel horse," he groaned. "I should've known!"

Lila and Jessica grinned at each other and walked away.

Donald sighed. One way or another he'd win these girls over. He'd get them to teach him some moves and he'd get on the boys' team. Donald Zwerdling was not going to remain a geek forever.

"When are they going to have the awards ceremony?" Jessica asked impatiently, looking at her watch.

Amy laughed. "There are still kids who haven't performed yet, Jessica," she said.

Jessica sighed. It wasn't like any of these kids were going to beat her scores anyway. The first-place trophy was hers!

"Is that Dawn Maven over by the uneven bars?" Lila asked.

Jessica turned. The petite, dark-haired girl was wringing her hands nervously.

Melissa McCormick patted Jessica on the back. "I hear Dawn Maven is Weston Middle School's Jessica Wakefield."

Jessica tossed her hair. "Well, *Weston's* Jessica Wakefield can't possibly be as great as the *real* Jessica Wakefield," she said, watching Dawn Maven out of the corner of her eye.

Dawn glanced at Jessica and frowned. *Probably because she's so obviously outclassed here,* Jessica thought. It couldn't be easy to be the best in your school and then go and compete someplace where you were suddenly *not* the best anymore.

As Dawn mounted the low bar, Jessica took a few steps closer for a better view. Dawn wasn't bad, Jessica had to admit. But of course, *she* was much better.

"She's really elegant, isn't she?" Amy said as they watched Dawn's free hip circle.

Jessica wrinkled her nose. Maybe Dawn *was* kind of elegant, but the uneven parallel bars wasn't about elegance. It was about flair. And Jessica Wakefield was the Queen of Flair.

Amy sucked in her breath. "Wow, she does a pirouette on the high bar!"

Jessica stared at Amy. Whose side was she on, anyway? "I do a pirouette too, you know," she said, her arms crossed.

Amy blinked. "Yeah, I know. But until now, you were the only person I knew who did one."

Jessica scowled. *Her* pirouette was way better than Dawn's. Her own teammate should've been able to see that.

But as Dawn came down in a simple straddle underswing, Jessica felt a knot in her stomach. *Come on,* Jessica told herself firmly. *It's not like she could have scored higher than a 9.7.* Still, she *was* a little nervous as she waited for the judges to evaluate Dawn's performance.

As the head judge held up Dawn's score, Jessica let out the breath she didn't realize she'd been holding. Dawn received a 9.4.

Jessica grabbed Amy. "We're going to the

California Games!" she yelled, jumping up and down.

"We're going to the California Games!" Amy cried.

The rest of the team ran up from the bench and joined them in one mass huddle. It was the most exciting afternoon of Jessica's life. Her team was going to the California Games, and they were going because of *her!*

"In second place, from Weston Middle School, Dawn Maven," announced one of the judges.

Jessica watched as Dawn walked to the three-step podium to receive her award. She walked slowly, with her shoulders slumped, as though she were going to a funeral. *What's she so bummed out about?* Jessica wondered. Second place at a meet that included Jessica Wakefield was pretty darn good.

Dawn raised her head long enough to shake hands with the third-place winner, who was also from Weston, then dragged herself up to the second step, where she dropped her head once more.

"And in first place—"

Jessica beamed as her teammates began to stamp their feet in a drumroll for her.

"From Sweet Valley Middle School, Jessica Wakefield!"

"All right, Jessica!" Mary Wallace cried.

The bleachers erupted with cheers and whistles.

As she passed the third-place winner, Jessica held out her hand. She was about to congratulate her when she noticed a huge banner being unrolled high in the bleachers.

Jessica Wakefield Is #1!!!!

Jessica squealed with glee and waved to the seventh graders who held the banner.

She hopped up onto the first-place step and held out her hand to congratulate Dawn. But Dawn just rolled her eyes. "Forget it," she said, turning away and nearly slapping Jessica in the face with her dark curly ponytail.

Jessica's mouth dropped open. But before she could even collect her thoughts, the judge was moving toward them, handing out the awards.

"Nice job," he told Dawn as he handed her a red ribbon.

Dawn frowned as she snatched it away.

Jessica looked at Dawn in disbelief, but only for a second. She had more important things to focus on—like the beautiful blue ribbon the judge was holding out to her.

"Nice job," the judge told her.

Nice job? Jessica repeated to herself. She couldn't help feeling a little disappointed he didn't say something more. Something like, "In all my years of judging gymnastics meets, yours was the most incredible bar routine I've ever seen."

Oh, well, Jessica told herself. *So what if he doesn't recognize pure genius when he sees it.*

The important thing was that she held the blue ribbon in her hand—her team's ticket to the California Games.

THREE

"I think you should print something about how Dawn Maven didn't even congratulate me," Jessica whispered to Elizabeth, who was taking notes for an upcoming *Sixers* article.

"Shhh!" Elizabeth held her finger to her lips. "I'm trying to hear."

It was Monday morning and the principal, Mr. Clark, had called a special school assembly in honor of Jessica. Well, Jessica had to admit he was talking about the upcoming California Games too, but everybody knew the girls' gymnastics team wouldn't even be going to the Games if it wasn't for her.

Jessica leaned over to see what Elizabeth was writing, but Elizabeth suddenly clasped her notebook to her chest.

"What? I just want to see what you're saying about me," Jessica explained.

Elizabeth sighed. "I'm not saying anything about you. I'm trying to get some of the history behind the California Games."

Jessica rolled her eyes. If you asked her, people would be a lot more interested in *her* history and how she came to be such a fabulous gymnast than in the history of the California Games. She shifted in her seat and tried to pay attention to Mr. Clark.

"Back in the 1950s, the top twenty-five middle school and junior high athletic teams in the state met once a year to compete in Los Angeles," Mr. Clark said. Jessica could tell he was reading from his notes. He wasn't just talking, like Mr. Bowman said you were supposed to do when you gave a speech.

"But because of budget cuts, the Games are only being held every other year now," Mr. Clark went on. "So it's quite an honor to get there."

Yeah, yeah, Jessica thought impatiently. *Get to the stuff about me!*

"This school has sent several soccer teams to the Games over the years. And we've sent a basketball team and a field hockey team. But Sweet Valley Middle School has never sent a girls' gymnastics team to the California Games."

"Are you getting this?" Jessica nudged Elizabeth.

"Yes!" Elizabeth murmured impatiently.

"But this year, thanks to an incredible performance on the uneven parallel bars by our own Jessica Wakefield, I'm proud to announce that Sweet Valley Middle School is sending their girls' gymnastics team to the California Games!"

Finally! Jessica thought as the gymnasium erupted

in applause. Without thinking, she stood up and took a bow. Mr. Clark hadn't asked her to, of course, but obviously she had a lot of adoring fans out there. She had to show her appreciation, didn't she?

"How late will you practice tonight, Jessica?" Elizabeth asked as they filed out of the auditorium after the assembly. "I was thinking I'd come to the gym and get some photos for the special California Games edition of the *Sixers*."

"We don't have practice tonight," Jessica replied. "We've got another meet with Weston. This time it's in their gym."

A girl Jessica didn't know turned around and smiled brightly. "Another meet? Good luck!"

"Luck?" another girl responded. "She doesn't need luck. She's Jessica Wakefield!"

"Where's Jessica Wakefield?" a third girl with glasses asked.

The other two pointed to Jessica.

"Oh wow!" The girl gazed at Jessica, wide-eyed. "Could I have your autograph?" she asked, thrusting a book at her.

Jessica stared at the book. It was a *science* book. "You want me to write in this?" she asked incredulously.

The girl blushed. "I would have brought my autograph book from home if I'd have known I'd run into you, but—"

"It's OK," Jessica cut in quickly. She put her foot up on a chair for balance and opened the book. A science book definitely wasn't the most glamorous place for her autograph, but she figured she had a responsibility to her fans.

"Hurry up, Jessica!" Elizabeth said as Jessica scrawled her name. "You're going to be late for math!"

Jessica sighed. How could a celebrity like herself be expected to worry about math class?

Dawn Maven pointed and flexed her feet to stretch her lower leg muscles. She was always nervous before a meet, but today she was even more nervous than usual. In order to make it to the California Games, Weston had to win either today's meet or Thursday's meet against Sweet Valley. And Dawn was going to see to it that they did.

Weston was supposed to be among the top teams in California. Dawn almost always won a blue ribbon for the team, but lately the rest of the team hadn't been pulling their weight. If they weren't careful, they weren't even going to qualify for the California Games. *And all these years of practice will have been for nothing,* Dawn thought.

Dawn watched as Jessica Wakefield entered her gym, then hurried toward her teammates, her long blond hair flowing freely behind her.

Several of Jessica's teammates crowded around her and they all started talking at once. Jessica flipped her beautiful hair over her shoulder and laughed.

Dawn's face burned. It wasn't fair. Jessica wasn't just a good gymnast. She wasn't just pretty. She was obviously really popular too. It seemed like she had it all.

Well, I'll fix her, Dawn said to herself. *I'll fix her good!*

"Kara?" Dawn said to her teammate. She leaned over

to massage her ankle as though it were really throbbing. "My ankle is still bothering me a little. Would you tell the coach I went to the locker room to wrap it?"

"You're going to wrap it now?" Kara asked. "The meet's going to start any minute!"

"I have to," Dawn insisted. Before Kara could say another word, Dawn stood up and limped across the gym. Once she reached the hallway, she looked both ways, then ran across to the locker room.

Dawn's heart pounded as she spun the combination on her lock. She opened her locker and pulled out a small paper bag. She'd been carrying the bag to meets for weeks now, but she'd never had the guts to use it before. And she'd never really needed to. She usually came out on top.

But her team had dragged her down one too many times. Things were getting down to the wire now. They needed this win if they were going to make it to the California Games.

Dawn set the bag down and pulled an old, worn Ace bandage out of her locker. She sat down on the hard wooden bench, took off her sock, and quickly wrapped her ankle.

Next, Dawn grabbed a bottle of baby oil from her bag. Being careful not to get any on her hands, she squeezed a blob of oil inside the bandage.

The oil felt cool against her skin. Dawn adjusted her bandage, feeling it to make absolutely sure the oil wouldn't show through.

She quickly recapped her bottle of oil and put it back in her locker. *Just try and get a nine point seven today, Jessica Wakefield,* Dawn said to herself.

And as she passed the mirrors on her way out, Dawn couldn't help but smile.

Jessica leaped to the high bar, then raised herself to a front support. She felt good today. Almost as good as she did at the last meet. And this was only her warm-up. She spun a few circles on the high bar and came down in a perfect somersault dismount.

"Jessica?" Coach Arlin called. "Could you come over here? I want to talk to you for a minute."

She looks so serious, Jessica thought as she wiped her forehead with a towel. What could Coach Arlin possibly have seen in her practice session to complain about?

She probably just wants to wish me luck, Jessica decided as she walked across the gym to where Coach Arlin was standing.

Coach Arlin put her hand on Jessica's shoulder. "I want you to watch Dawn Maven carefully today," she said.

Jessica frowned. She scored 9.7 on the uneven bars, and Coach Arlin wanted her to watch somebody else? "No offense, Ms. Arlin," she said. "But I'm already great."

Coach Arlin smiled faintly. "Watch when Dawn makes her turns. She's incredibly graceful. You might learn something."

Jessica watched as her coach walked away. What was Coach Arlin talking about? So what if Dawn had beautiful turns? Jessica was the one who made awesome changes from one bar to the next. Maybe Dawn would learn something from watching *her*.

As Jessica slipped her grips off, she glanced casually at Dawn, who strode over to the uneven parallel bars with her nose in the air.

Jessica noticed that her ankle was wrapped, but as Dawn mounted the low bar and practiced some circles, she didn't look as if she was in any pain at all. Her body was absolutely straight on the swings and perfectly tucked on the spins.

Jessica shook her head. Dawn may look good, but there was no way she was going to beat Jessica today. No way at all.

The buzzer sounded, indicating practice time was over, and Dawn came down in a layaway dismount. She strutted past Jessica like she owned the world. "May the best woman win!" she said with a smirk.

Jessica stared at her dark ponytail as it swished from side to side. "The best woman will," she called after Dawn. "Count on it!"

"Next on the uneven parallel bars . . . Dawn Maven," the judge called.

And after Dawn, it's me, Jessica thought. She was glad Dawn was up first. That way Jessica would know what she had to beat.

Dawn put on her grips and chalked them up really well. She raised her hands to the judges and then mounted the low bar.

Up and around, back and over she swung. With every move, her legs were together and her body was at the exact angle it should be.

Jessica had to admit, Dawn was good—but she wasn't perfect. When Dawn did her pirouette, Jessica noticed she didn't move her first hand down the bar the way she was supposed to. So when she came out of the pirouette, she was way over to the side. It wasn't something that would be counted as a deduction. But she spent the next couple of moves inching back to the middle of the bar, which in Jessica's opinion was *far* from graceful.

Dawn came down in her straddle dismount, and the crowd, which was made up mostly of Weston fans, stamped and cheered.

Dawn raised her hands to the judges and then bent down to massage her ankle. When she stood up, she smiled menacingly at Jessica and ran her hand back and forth along the low bar.

She acts like she owns the entire apparatus, Jessica thought with annoyance.

She waited for Dawn's score before heading over to the bars herself. The judge held it over his head: 9.5.

Jessica felt a knot in her stomach. *But I can do even better,* she told herself firmly. *Remember, you're Jessica Wakefield.*

Here goes, Jessica thought as she mounted the low bar at the start of her routine.

But right away, when she turned that first clear hip circle, Jessica could tell something was wrong. Her hands felt sweaty, like she didn't have a good grip.

I should've taken more time with the chalk, she thought as she squatted on the low bar and leaped to the high bar. But she almost missed it. Her left hand slipped off the bar and she had to compensate for that by grabbing harder with her right hand. What was going on?

Her blind back-straddle was next. If she couldn't grab the bar going forward, how was she going to grab it going backward? *You're just going to have to,* she told herself as she spit a stray hair out of her mouth. She held her breath and released the top bar.

Bang! Her hands came down firmly on the low bar, just the way they were supposed to. But again, they felt slippery. Out of control. Now her breathing was out of control too.

I'm going to fall! she thought desperately.

Her heart was pounding. Her face burned. If only she could get down and clean her grips. Put on more chalk. But she knew that she couldn't.

Back to the high bar. This time she held on, but just barely. Jessica had no idea she had so much strength in the tips of her fingers.

Her handstand and pirouette were next. Jessica felt panic rising in her throat. And she knew better than to attempt a handstand and pirouette on the high bar. So instead she did a straddle underswing dismount—and not even a very good one. She had to take an extra step on her landing.

She blinked back her tears as she slowly raised her hands to the judges.

Unable to look at her teammates, she walked away from the apparatus. *I don't understand,* she thought as she unfastened her grips. *How could I have—?* At that moment, she felt something strange on the outside of her grips. Her forehead wrinkled in confusion, she looked down at the grips and ran a finger across the fabric. Her grips were coated with oil!

FOUR

"What happened out there?" Coach Arlin asked with concern as Jessica returned to the bench.

"Yeah, how could you screw up like that?" Lila demanded.

Donald handed her a towel and Jessica yanked it away from him without saying a word. Her whole body was shaking with rage. Where had that oil come from?

Coach Arlin squeezed Jessica's elbow. "Jessica—"

"Shhh! They're getting ready to announce her score!" Lila hissed.

Jessica's heart froze, and she shut her eyes tightly. *Please be lenient,* she begged the judges silently. *Please realize it wasn't my fault. . . .*

"5.3!" the head judge announced.

"5.3?" Amy whispered with shock.

Jessica dropped her head to her hands. The

humiliation was almost more than she could bear.

Coach Arlin sighed heavily. "Well, Jessica, everyone has an off day sometimes. The important thing now is to—"

"I'm not having an *off day!*" Jessica cried, snapping her head up. "Somebody put oil on the bars!"

Lila frowned. "Oil?" she asked skeptically.

"Yes!" Jessica insisted. "The bars were slippery. Look at my grips!" She held them out. "They're caked with oil!"

Lila sniffed. "Then why didn't you clean them before you got up on the bars?"

"Because they weren't oily then!" Jessica stomped her foot. "I'm telling you, somebody purposely sabotaged my routine."

"Jessica," Coach Arlin said gently, brushing some wisps of hair from Jessica's forehead. "I'm sorry you had a bad day, but you can't make accusations like that. Especially in somebody else's gym. We could be disqualified for poor sportsmanship."

"*We* could be disqualified?" Jessica stared wide-eyed at her coach. "What about the person who did this to me?"

Amy Sutton crossed her arms. "And who would do such a thing?" she asked.

Jessica scanned the row of Weston gymnasts. She didn't really know any of them personally. "It could've been any one of them," she said with a wave of her hand.

Then Jessica noticed Dawn Maven wiping the bars with her towel. "No, wait!" she said, drawing in her breath. "It was *her*." She pointed at Dawn. "I beat her last Friday and she wanted to make sure I didn't beat her again. So she put oil on the bars. And look! Now she's wiping it off!"

Amy, Lila, and Coach Arlin turned around to look.

"She's just wiping the chalk off the bar," Amy said.

"Then why is she scrubbing so hard?" Jessica asked.

"Dawn performed right before you did, Jessica," Coach Arlin reminded her. "How could she have put oil on the bars between your performances?"

Jessica's eyes traveled down Dawn's leg to her bandaged ankle. "I remember!" Jessica bounced to her feet. "Right after her score came up, she bent down and rubbed her sore ankle. Then right after that, she ran her hand over the bar."

Amy and Lila looked doubtful.

Coach Arlin pursed her lips.

Jessica crossed her arms and glared at Dawn. "I bet her ankle isn't even hurt," she said suspiciously. "She just used that bandage to hide a handful of oil! I say we go right over there and demand she take off that bandage this instant!"

Coach Arlin gripped Jessica by the arms. "Listen to yourself. Do you have any idea how ridiculous you sound? We can't go over there and accuse that poor girl of faking an injury just so she could somehow sabotage your routine."

"But that's what happened!" Jessica insisted. Her eyes swelled with tears again. Why wouldn't they believe her?

Coach Arlin's face softened. She wrapped her arms around Jessica.

Jessica buried her face in her coach's jacket and

let the tears flow. After a few minutes, she raised her eyes and glanced over Coach Arlin's shoulder. Dawn Maven was looking right at her.

Dawn smiled sweetly, then spun on her heel and turned away.

"You have to put this meet behind you and concentrate on the next one," Coach Arlin told Jessica, handing her a tissue.

"Or concentrate on the California Games," Amy offered, patting Jessica on the back. "We're still going, you know."

Jessica nodded and forced a smile. She dried her eyes. "You guys are right," she said. "There are other things I should be concentrating on."

Namely *revenge*, she thought as she narrowed her eyes at Dawn.

"You'll never guess what happened at volleyball today, Jess!" Elizabeth cried as she burst into the kitchen.

Jessica glanced up from her half-melted ice cream. Her sister looked like she'd run all the way home. Long strands of her blond hair had escaped from her ponytail, and her face was fire-engine red.

"A team of aliens landed in the gym and you beat them?" Jessica suggested.

"Nope!" Elizabeth laughed as she sank into the chair across from Jessica. "Guess again."

Jessica sighed. She was in no mood for guessing games. Her mind was on one thing: how to pay Dawn back for what she did.

"Well?" Elizabeth pressed.

" 'Well' what?" Jessica mumbled.

"Oh, all right, I'll just tell you then," Elizabeth said excitedly, grabbing an apple from the basket on the table. "We just beat Weston Middle School—which means we're just three games away from the California Games. Wouldn't that be awesome, Jess, if we *both* made it?"

"Awesome," Jessica murmured distractedly. She stirred her ice cream, then looked up at her sister. "Elizabeth? If you wanted to cheat in volleyball, how would you do it?"

"Cheat?" Elizabeth stared at Jessica as though she'd never even heard the word. "Why would anybody want to cheat?"

"Never mind," Jessica sighed. She should've known Elizabeth wouldn't understand.

"Think fast!" Steven Wakefield, Jessica's fourteen-year-old brother, threw his basketball to her just as she wandered outside to the driveway.

She caught it hard against her chest.

"Hey, what do you know?" Steven said with surprise. "She actually caught it!"

"Ha, ha," Jessica said as she tossed the ball back. She watched her brother shoot a basket and miss. Normally, she would have started teasing him, but now she thought better of it. "Hey, Steven?" she asked casually. "How would a person cheat in basketball?"

Steven trotted down the driveway after the basketball and dribbled it back. "There are lots of ways to cheat," he said. "Anything from flagrant fouling to putting sugar in the other team's towels." He aimed for the basket again, and with a *Whoosh,* the ball went in.

"Sugar?" Jessica wrinkled her nose in confusion as she grabbed the ball. "What does that do?"

"Well, if you get sugar on your hands and then you sweat, your hands will get all sticky," Steven explained. "It's pretty hard to make a decent pass with sticky hands."

It's pretty hard to hang onto a bar with sticky hands too, Jessica mused, holding the ball against her hip.

Steven knocked the ball out of her grasp. "Of course, if somebody did that to you, you'd just call time and wash it off." Jessica smiled as Steven sunk another basket. Maybe in basketball you'd call time, but not in gymnastics. There were no time-outs in gymnastics.

Jessica dropped the two five-pound bags of sugar she'd taken from the pantry onto her bed.

But now that she had the sugar, what was she going to do with it? How was she going to get it on Dawn's hands? She flopped down on her bed next to the two bags to think.

She could talk to Donald Zwerdling, their fabulous towel boy, and see if he'd make sure Dawn got the towel with the sugar in it.

But it was risky involving a geek like Donald. For one thing, he might say no. He might even tell the coach what Jessica wanted to do. And even if he did agree to do it, he might screw it up.

No, she had to do this herself.

Thursday's meet would be held in the Sweet Valley gym. It wouldn't be that weird if Jessica took a towel over to Dawn herself. But then Jessica remembered that it wasn't until after you performed that you needed a towel. What if the uneven parallel bars was the first apparatus that Dawn performed on? She wouldn't use the towel until *after* her performance. There had to be another way to get Dawn's hands sticky.

She couldn't just rub sugar on the bar the way Dawn had rubbed oil on it. Sugar wouldn't stick to the wood the way oil did. No, Jessica had to get the sugar on Dawn's *hands*. Or her *grips*. And she had to do it without Dawn suspecting.

The chalk tray! Jessica sat up straight. It was perfect! Chalk was white. So was sugar. It would blend right in. Dawn would put on her grips, spray them with water and then coat them with chalk. But somehow Jessica would see that the chalk had sugar in it too. Dawn's grips would have a sticky coating of water, chalk, and *sugar*. She'd mount the bar with that smug little look of hers, and with any luck at all, she'd fall flat on her turned-up little nose!

Jessica hugged herself as she thought of it. "I am an absolute genius," she said out loud.

FIVE

Donald sighed as once again he landed in a heap on the floor. He'd been trying to do a handspring for the last twenty minutes, with no luck at all. But he wasn't going to give up.

He'd been watching the girls when they practiced their floor routines. Lila's began with a little dance sort of thing, then she turned and did three walkovers right in time with the music.

Walkovers, not handsprings, Donald reminded himself. A handspring had a lift to it. He'd read that in a gymnastics book he'd borrowed from the library. A handspring was what Donald's first Donald Zwerdling Zzzpecial had been. But he hadn't been able to do one since that day in the boys' gym.

Donald watched as Lila practiced her walkovers on the next mat. She took a step forward, went down into a handstand and over, all in one smooth movement.

Step, hands down, and over, Donald said to himself. He stood up and went to the edge of the mat to try it.

Step, hands down and over. You can do it. Donald took a step, stretched his hands down to the mat, kicked his legs up behind him, and fell flat on his face.

Lila snorted in laughter.

That's a very strange sound to come out of her nose, considering how popular she is, Donald thought. But he decided to keep that knowledge to himself. He'd save it for sometime when Lila *really* got on his nerves.

"Exactly what was that supposed to be?" Lila asked.

Donald jumped to his feet. "It's my Donald Zwerdling Zzzpecial," he said with pride.

Lila looked skeptical. "And what exactly is this Donald Zwerdling Zzzpecial thing again?"

"Well, I've changed it. The new and improved Donald Zwerdling Zzzpecial is where I do walkover after walkover all around the outer edges of the mat," Donald said, pleased that she was interested enough to ask. "Er, that's what it *will* be when I learn how to do it."

"Any mediocre gymnast can do that," Lila said, obviously unimpressed. "You can't name something after yourself when everybody else has already done it!"

"Sure I can," Donald said. He wasn't going to let Lila bring him down. "I'm not officially on any gymnastics team, so I can do whatever I want."

Lila rolled her eyes. "Whatever you say," she said. Then she went back to her own walkovers.

It took a few minutes before Donald realized Lila

was doing a series of walkovers all around the edge of the mat, just like he wanted to do. When she finished, she stuck her tongue out at him.

Donald didn't think she looked too pretty like that. But instead of saying so, he turned his attention back to his walkovers. *I'm going to do one of these things if it kills me,* he said to himself. He took a step, put his hands down, feet up and landed with a hard thud on his back. And as he lay there staring at the bright lights on the ceiling he wondered whether a front walkover *would* kill him.

Jessica sat on a bench in the locker room, sifting through the bag of sugar and tray of chalk. Her teammates were practicing, but right now, she had more important things to do.

Jessica studied the two white powdery substances. The sugar was more granular and shinier than the chalk. If she put too much in, Dawn would see it. But if she didn't put enough in, Dawn's grips wouldn't get sticky. How was she supposed to figure out the right amount? Neither the sugar nor the chalk came with directions for sabotaging someone's performance on the uneven parallel bars.

I guess I'll just have to experiment, Jessica decided. She went to the supply closet for a clean bucket. On her way, she peeked into the gym. Donald Zwerdling was prancing around the floor like a maniac. *Why doesn't he give it up?* Jessica wondered. *He has zero chance of ever getting anywhere in gymnastics.*

Unless . . . An idea was starting to take shape in Jessica's mind. One way that Donald Zwerdling might succeed in gymnastics was as a guinea pig. Her guinea pig.

Jessica hurried back to the locker room with her bucket and set it on the floor with a clang. First she dumped the chalk in. Then she added an equal amount of sugar and stirred it all together with her hand.

After hiding away the remaining bags of sugar and blocks of chalk in her locker, Jessica grabbed the bucket and hurried back to the gym. Melissa McCormick was on the balance beam and Lila was on the uneven bars. But she walked right past them and went straight to Donald Zwerdling, who was practicing on the floor.

It looked like he was attempting a handstand, but it was hard to tell. Jessica cringed as he fell flat on his face.

"I hate to tell you this, Donald," Jessica said. "But I don't think the floor exercise is your thing."

Donald raised his head to look at her. "I'm getting it," he said, dragging himself to a sitting position. "My Donald Zwerdling Zzzpecial is really coming along."

Jessica had to choke back a laugh. "I think you need a new Donald Zwerdling Zzzpecial," she told him. "And I know just the apparatus for you. The uneven parallel bars!"

Donald stared at her, his eyes wide.

"Come on," she said as she pulled him to his feet and dragged him over to the bars.

"But boys don't even compete on the uneven parallel bars," Donald argued.

"Well, maybe you can be the first," Jessica said as

she set the bucket down. They had to wait for Lila to finish on the bars before Donald could have a turn.

Lila did a layaway straddle dismount, and Donald stared at her in awe. Jessica waved her hand in front of his face to get his attention. "Here. The first thing you need is a pair of hand grips." She handed him her own grips.

Donald took them and turned them all around. "What are these dowels for?" he asked, pointing at a silver rod in the middle of the grip.

"It helps you get a better hold on the bar," Jessica explained. She grabbed one grip and held it between her knees as she took Donald's hand and squeezed his fingers through the holes in the other grip.

Lila came up behind Jessica. "What are you doing?" she asked.

"Just showing Donald a few simple moves on the bars," Jessica replied.

Lila stared at her like she was crazy. "What on earth for? We've got another meet against Weston in two days. Don't you think you should be getting ready for that?"

I am getting ready for the meet with Weston, Jessica thought. But she didn't dare say it. "Coach Arlin says we should help each other out," she said instead. "You know, teamwork."

Lila raised an eyebrow as if to say *it's your funeral.* Then she walked away.

Donald opened and closed his fingers. "This thing is pretty uncomfortable," he said.

"You'll get used to it," Jessica told him, working the other grip over Donald's left hand.

Jessica led Donald over to the chalk tray. "Now first we spray the plastic parts with water," Jessica said as she squirted water onto the grips. "That'll make the chalk stick."

Donald reached for the chalk, but Jessica pulled him back. "No, no, no! Use this chalk over here," she said, pointing to her bucket. "This chalk is much better for beginners."

"OK." Donald shrugged. He stuck his hands into Jessica's bucket and rubbed the chalk onto the grips.

"Now come over here and mount the low bar," Jessica instructed. "Just grab hold and pull yourself up. Like this!" She jumped up to a front support to show him, then hopped down. "Now you try it."

Donald placed his hands on the bar and jumped up. "Hey, this isn't bad," he said, wiggling his toes in little flutter kicks.

Jessica swatted his legs. "Stop that!" she said. "How does your grip feel?"

"I don't know," he replied, shifting his arms on the bar. "How *should* it feel?"

Jessica sighed. It was a simple question! "Does it feel like you've got a good grip or do your hands feel sticky, er, sweaty?"

"They feel fine," Donald said as he leaned over the bar and turned a front hip circle. His feet hit the mat with a thud.

"That was fun!" he exclaimed. "Let me try it again." He jumped up to a front support and turned another front hip circle.

Jessica tapped her foot, watching for any sign that the sugar was working.

This time Donald actually managed to pull himself back up to a front support. He grinned at Jessica. "This isn't bad. Maybe you were right, Jessica. Maybe I just needed a new apparatus."

Jessica frowned. The sugar didn't seem to affect Donald at all. She scratched her chin. "No, something doesn't look quite right," she said. "Maybe this chalk is old. Let me run and get you some more."

Before Donald could protest, she grabbed her bucket and hurried across the gym to the locker room.

She poured a little more sugar into the bucket, stirred it around with her hand and then hurried back to Donald, who was practicing more front hip circles.

"Here, try this chalk," Jessica said.

Donald jumped down and put his hands in the bucket. But when he got back on the bars, he still didn't seem to be having any trouble. His legs swung forward and back. He pulled one leg up and over the low bar and turned a mill circle. Then he pulled the other leg up so that he was sitting on the low bar.

Jessica frowned again. "Something still doesn't look right," she said, shaking her head. "I'll be right back."

She grabbed the bucket again and ran it back to the locker room where she added still *more* sugar. You could kind of see the sugar in the mixture now, if you looked closely. *Hopefully this will do the trick!* she thought.

Jessica ran back to the gym and once again Donald jumped down to dip his hands in the bucket.

This time when Donald hopped up on the bar, Jessica could see a definite difference. He seemed to be really struggling to hold on.

"Hey," he said, shifting his grip. "Something doesn't feel right." Then he lost his grip altogether and crashed to the mat.

Jessica hid her smile behind her hand. "You're doing just fine, Donald," she said. "Just fine."

"Jess-ica! Jess-ica!" the crowd chanted as Jessica completed her routine on the uneven parallel bars. It was the last meet before the California Games, and the Sweet Valley Middle School bleachers were more packed than ever before.

Jessica raised her hands to the judges, then waved to the crowd, who cheered even louder when the judges revealed Jessica's score: 9.5.

Jessica's heart leaped. Her routine had been nearly perfect, but that wasn't the only reason she was excited. From the corner of her eye, she could see Dawn approaching. Jessica couldn't have hoped for a better lineup today. She had been first on the bars and Dawn was second. Now it was time to put her plan into action.

Picturing the chalk tray in her mind, Jessica backed away from the apparatus, still waving to her public. With one violent step she upset the chalk tray, and all the chalk spilled onto the floor.

She spun around. "Oh my," she said, putting a hand to her mouth as the head judge cast a disapproving glance at her. "I don't know how that could've happened."

Dawn rolled her eyes. "You are such a clod," she said.

Jessica put on a fake smile. *Yes, terrible, aren't I?*

she thought. "I'll go get some more chalk," she said out loud.

"That's OK. I'll do it!" Donald Zwerdling seemed to appear out of nowhere.

"No!" Jessica cried. "*I'll* do it. After all, I'm the one who knocked the tray over."

"But that's my job," Donald insisted. "I'm the towel boy, remember?"

Jessica grabbed a towel from the floor and tossed it at Donald. "So towel up the mess," she said through gritted teeth. She picked up the tray. "And *I'll* go get the chalk." Before Donald could protest any more, she hurried out of the gym and into the locker room, where she retrieved the bucket of chalk and sugar she'd mixed the other day for Donald. Quickly she poured some of the mixture into the tray.

"Here we are," she said once she returned to the gym with the tray. She set it back in place. "Break a leg, Dawn," she added sweetly.

With a glare at Jessica, Dawn put her hands into the mixture.

Grinning, Jessica returned to her bench to watch the show.

"Dawn doesn't look so great today," Amy Sutton whispered in Jessica's ear.

A smile slowly spread across Jessica's face. "No, she doesn't, does she?"

Jessica was pleased to see how well the sugar was working. Dawn's movements weren't quite as controlled today. Her thigh rammed against the bar on her free hip. She wouldn't get credit for the move.

And then when she leaped to the high bar, she almost missed it. *Now she knows how I felt last Friday,* Jessica thought with satisfaction.

Dawn's handstand was next. Jessica watched breathlessly as she swung up, but she didn't swing quite high enough. It seemed as if it was all she could do just to hold onto the bar.

Then, all of a sudden, her hand slipped and her body crashed to the mat with a thud. The gym filled with gasps.

"Aw, what a shame," Jessica murmured, biting back her smile. *That'll teach you to mess with Jessica Wakefield,* she thought.

"I think she's really hurt," Amy said with concern.

"I'm sure she's fine." Jessica waved her hand dismissively.

"She's not getting up." Mary Wallace stood up to get a better view.

"And look, there goes her coach." Amy pointed.

Jessica watched as Dawn's coach, Mr. Wykoff, ran out to where Dawn lay in a heap on the mat.

"My leg!" Dawn screamed as she pulled on her leg. Tears streamed down her face.

Coach Wykoff said something to her and she shook her head. Eventually he picked her up and carried her to the bench.

"Boy, talk about playing up the sympathy," Jessica muttered.

When Dawn's score was announced, Dawn buried her face in her hands and sobbed. It was a 2.0.

Jessica grunted. In her opinion, that was generous!

"Well," Jessica said, rubbing her hands together. "I guess that makes *me* the winner today."

"Too bad this isn't the California Games," Lila remarked. "You'd be taking home a gold medal instead of just another blue ribbon."

"I'll be taking home the gold medal anyway," Jessica said confidently. She glanced over at Dawn, who was seated at the end of the bench with her back to everyone. Her left ankle was wrapped in ice and propped up on a chair.

She isn't really that hurt, is she? Jessica wondered. *No, she can't be. She's probably faking it just to get attention.*

"Well, wish me luck." Lila stood up. "I'm up next on the bars."

On the bars? Jessica thought with alarm. She'd forgotten other people would be using the bars after Dawn. She couldn't let somebody from her own team dust her hands with that chalk.

"Wait!" Jessica cried. "I think we need new chalk."

Lila raised an eyebrow. "You just refilled it."

But Jessica ignored her. She ran over to the bars and grabbed the chalk tray.

"Excuse me!" the head judge called. He was an older man with white hair and wire-rimmed glasses. "Only competitors and coaches are allowed on the floor during competition."

"I'm just going to replace the chalk," Jessica explained.

"Didn't you replace the chalk before our last competitor?" he asked.

"Yes, she did," the other judge piped up. She was

a fairly young woman, and she wore her long blond hair piled on her head.

Jessica's heart pounded. If anybody suspected her of foul play, her team would be disqualified. But she *couldn't* let Lila use this chalk.

"I uh, never actually put more in," she said. "When I got to the hall, I noticed there was quite a bit of chalk that didn't spill, so I just put the tray back. But now it's *really* low." Jessica backed slowly toward the door. Hopefully neither of the judges would stand up and actually look in the tray. There was plenty of chalk inside. Chalk and *sugar*.

The judges exchanged a glance. Finally the head judge waved her off. "Hurry up with it!" he said.

Dawn looked up at Jessica with suspicion. But Jessica just waved cheerfully. *OK, Dawn*, she thought. *Now we're even*.

SIX

Jessica's feet hit the mat with a thud. "Well?" she asked, turning to face her coach. "What do you think?"

Coach Arlin scratched her forehead. "Not bad," she said.

"*Not bad?*" Jessica said with disappointment. She expected Coach Arlin to say, "Why Jessica, that was an amazing double flyaway and you'd be crazy not to try it at the California Games!"

Coach Arlin nodded. "I think you'll be ready to do it in competition next season."

"Next *season!*" Jessica stomped her foot. "I want to do it in competition *now*. I want to do it at the California Games!"

"Jessica, the California Games are only a week away," Coach Arlin reminded her. "It's not a good idea to change your routine so close to competition."

Jessica put her hands on her hips. "This isn't just a competition, this is the California Games. I don't want to do the same old boring routine. I want to do something special. I want to leave my mark!"

Coach Arlin wrinkled her forehead in confusion. "But your flyaway is perfect. Your entire routine is perfect. If you change to the double flyaway and you make a mistake, you can forget about bringing home a medal."

"And if I *don't* make a mistake, I could bring home the gold," Jessica pointed out.

Coach Arlin sighed. "Well, if that's the way you feel, we've got work to do. Get back up there and try it again."

"Wow, that was terrific!" Elizabeth applauded Amy as she dismounted the balance beam.

Amy grinned. "Thanks." She grabbed a towel and wiped her face. "What are you doing here?"

"I just got out of volleyball practice and I was wondering if Jessica wanted to walk home with me." Elizabeth looked around. "Do you know where she is?"

"She's on the bars," Amy said, pointing.

"Hey Elizabeth!" Donald Zwerdling called from across the gym. "I'm going to attempt a brand new Donald Zwerdling Zzzpecial. How would you like to be the first to witness this great event?"

Elizabeth laughed. "What exactly is a Donald Zwerdling Zzzpecial?" she asked, turning to face Donald.

"Oh, don't encourage him," Amy moaned.

"Why not?" Elizabeth asked. It seemed to her

everybody could use a little encouragement.

"Come on. You'll see." Donald waved as he went to stand by the balance beam. Melissa McCormick was on the beam, but Donald waited patiently below.

"I thought your Donald Zwerdling Zzzpecial was something you did on the uneven parallel bars," Amy said, trailing behind Elizabeth.

"The uneven parallel bars!" Donald cried. "Are you nuts? I can't compete with *her*," he said, nodding toward Jessica. "No, I've given up the uneven parallel bars for the balance beam."

Melissa turned three cartwheels along the length of the beam, then came down in a roundoff dismount.

"Good job, Melissa!" Amy yelled.

Donald swallowed. "Yeah, you're going to be a hard act to follow," he said.

Melissa smiled politely. "Gee, thanks, Donald," she said.

"OK, Elizabeth. Get ready for the sight of the century," Donald said. He walked over to the beam and raised himself up to a front support.

"I didn't think boys competed on the balance beam," Elizabeth whispered to Amy.

Amy smiled as Donald swung his leg over the beam and rose awkwardly to his feet. "Let's just say Donald isn't your average gymnast," she said.

Donald airplaned his arms out to the sides and teetered back and forth. "So far, so good!" He grinned at Elizabeth and Amy. "OK, here I go." He did a lunge, then a hop, and then he spun around on one foot, lost his balance, and jumped to the floor. "Oops," he said, glancing sheepishly at Elizabeth.

"That wasn't quite right. Let me try it again."

"Actually, Donald—" Amy began before Donald could mount the beam again. "I really need to practice my routine. Maybe you could show us your Donald Zwerdling Zzzpecial another time."

Donald's face fell. "Well, OK," he said. "Maybe I'll go try the vault."

Elizabeth looked at her friend with surprise. Amy had already had lots of time on the beam. "Maybe you should have given him another chance to get it right," Elizabeth said. "It seems really important to him."

Amy shook her head. "Believe me, I did him a favor kicking him off now, before he killed himself."

"Did you feel the difference that time?" Coach Arlin asked Jessica. "You came through the bottom of your swing much better and you kept your body nice and tight during the turns."

Jessica nodded. "I told you I'd get it in time for the California Games."

Coach Arlin smiled. "Yes, you did," she agreed. "Keep up that attitude and you just might bring home a medal!"

Not just any medal, Jessica thought as Coach Arlin walked away. She was going to bring home the *gold* medal.

Jessica could see it now. Everyone in the entire arena would be staring only at her, amazed at how fearlessly she leaped from one bar to the other. When she got ready for her double flyaway dismount, some people would be too scared to watch. Others wouldn't be able to stop themselves from staring as her body came away from the high bar, swung two perfect circles, and came to land square on the mat. There would be a collective sigh of relief, then everyone would stand up, yelling and cheering, "Jess-ica! Jess-ica! Jess-ica!"

"Jessica!" Melissa McCormick interrupted her thoughts.

"What?" Jessica asked with annoyance.

"You're just standing there. If you're done, I'd like to practice my routine."

Jessica sighed. "I guess I'm done." She grabbed her towel and went to get a drink of water. As she passed the bleachers, she noticed a couple of girls watching her. They looked like they were from the elementary school. Sometimes younger girls came over to watch the middle school team practice.

"I think that's Jessica Wakefield," a girl with short brown hair whispered to a girl with a red braid as Jessica walked by.

"Oh, wow," Red Braid said. "She's going to win in the California Games, you know. Especially now that that girl from Weston is out of the running."

Jessica's head spun around. "What did you say?" she asked.

The girl's eyes widened and she swallowed hard as Jessica took a step closer to her. It was as if she could hardly believe somebody of Jessica's stature would bother to speak to her.

"What girl from Weston?" Jessica demanded.

"Um, the *good* one," the girl replied, playing with her braid. "Didn't you know she got hurt at the last meet?"

"She's not that hurt," Jessica protested. "She'll be fine for the California Games."

"I don't know," the brown-haired girl said. "My baby-sitter goes to Weston and she said that girl came to school on *crutches* today. She could hardly walk."

There was an empty feeling in the pit of Jessica's stomach. It wasn't true, was it? Dawn couldn't have gotten *that* hurt?

No, these were elementary school kids. They were going by what a baby-sitter told them. And they could've gotten what the baby-sitter said totally mixed up.

Jessica continued on to the drinking fountain. No, she told herself firmly. *These kids don't know what they're talking about.*

"Everybody's been talking about you all day, Jessica," Elizabeth said during dinner that night.

Jessica's fork clattered to the floor. Had somebody found out what she did to Dawn? "What do you mean they've been talking about me? What have they been saying?" she asked, her voice rising with panic.

Elizabeth laughed. "Just stuff about how you're going to bring home a gold medal at the California Games."

"Relax, honey," Mrs. Wakefield said to Jessica as she bent down to retrieve her fork. "I think the pressures of the California Games are getting to you."

"Nah, it's just all the time she spends hanging upside down from the uneven parallel bars," Steven said. "The oxygen collects in her brain and makes her even nuttier than usual."

"Ha ha," Jessica said, making a face at her brother. She didn't have the energy to come up with a better response.

"Don't give your sister a hard time, Steven," Mr. Wakefield said.

"Yeah," Elizabeth put in. "Jess has been working really hard. And it's because of her that Sweet Valley is even able to send a gymnastics team to the California Games."

Steven rolled his eyes. "Maybe they'll build a shrine in her honor."

"Maybe they will." Jessica smiled faintly. She was starting to breathe a little more easily now. It looked like no one thought she had anything to do with Dawn's injuries.

"Oops, the sugar bowl is empty," Mrs. Wakefield said as she held the small lid in her hand.

"I'll go refill it," Elizabeth offered, scooting her chair back from the table.

Mrs. Wakefield handed the sugar bowl to Elizabeth. "Thank you, honey."

Jessica moved the rice and pieces of fish around on her plate to make it look like she'd eaten more than she had. She was usually famished after gymnastics practice, but for some reason, she just wasn't very hungry tonight.

"Hey, Mom?" Elizabeth poked her head back into the dining room. "There isn't any more sugar in the pantry."

Jessica's heart stopped. "That's OK," she spoke up quickly. "We don't need sugar on our berries. It's healthier to eat them plain. Right, Mom?"

Mrs. Wakefield gave her a small smile. "Well, I suppose—"

"I know there's sugar in there," Mr. Wakefield broke in with a frown. "I just bought two bags last week. Did you look behind the cereal?"

"I looked everywhere," Elizabeth said.

Mr. Wakefield dabbed the corner of his mouth with his napkin. "That's strange. How could two bags of sugar just up and—"

"Hey, do you remember that TV special about this sort of thing?" Jessica cut in. "*Mysterious Disappearances of Household Goods,* or something like that? It was all about this exact, um, phenomenon. You buy sugar, and poof, it's gone!"

Steven knit his brows as he shoveled more food into his mouth. "What are you—"

"Well, we're lucky, actually, because we all need to cut back on sugar anyway," Jessica continued. "Some people lose stuff like milk and bread and toothpaste." She looked cautiously at Steven, praying he wouldn't mention the conversation they had the other day about sugar and cheating.

But Steven just looked at Jessica as if she was crazy. "That's the most bizarre thing I ever heard of."

"Isn't it?" Jessica laughed lightly. "Imagine. What would anyone want with toothpaste?"

"I kno-o-o-ow wha-a-a-at you di-i-i-id! I kno-o-o-ow wha-a-a-at you di-i-i-id!"

Jessica ran through the halls at school, but everywhere she went she saw Dawn Maven's distorted face and heard those same words, "I kno-o-o-ow wha-a-a-at you di-i-i-id! I kno-o-o-ow wha-a-a-at you di-i-i-id!"

Jessica opened her locker. Dawn's elongated face stared at her from the inside wall. *"I kno-o-o-ow wha-a-a-at you di-i-i-id! I kno-o-o-ow wha-a-a-at you di-i-i-id!"*

Jessica screamed and dropped the books she didn't even know she was carrying. She ran down the hall toward the school exit. But the door was chained shut. And on the glass was Dawn's face, fat this time. *"I kno-o-o-ow wha-a-a-at you di-i-i-id! I kno-o-o-ow wha-a-a-at you di-i-i-id!"*

"No!" Jessica cried. *"Leave me alone!"*

Jessica bolted up in bed. Her breath was coming in short gasps.

There were streaks of light shining through the closed blinds on her window. Jessica turned to her bedside clock. It was 8:12 A.M. on Saturday. It had all been a dream.

She fell back against her pillows. *Just a dream,* she told herself.

Her breathing slowed and she closed her eyes.

Just as she was about to drop off to sleep again, the telephone rang.

"What!" Jessica cried as she bolted up in bed once again.

Somebody knows! she thought fearfully. Somebody knew, and now they were calling to tell her not to bother showing up for gymnastics practice anymore. She was through with gymnastics. Forever!

Jessica tossed her covers aside and tiptoed to her

door. She could hear her dad's voice. "I'll have my secretary fax those papers to you first thing Monday morning." Jessica breathed another sigh of relief as she silently closed her door. It was just one of her dad's clients.

There wasn't any point trying to get back to sleep now. Jessica went to her closet and pulled out her warm-up suit. *Might as well head up to the school a little early and get some extra practice in,* she thought. Maybe it would take her mind off Dawn.

After all, there's nothing to feel guilty about, she told herself. Dawn was the one who started this whole thing. All Jessica had done was even the score.

Jessica dropped her gym bag on the patio and flopped down on a lounge chair. "Boy am I beat," she said, draping a hand across her forehead.

Elizabeth glanced up from her notebook. "Have you been at the gym all morning?" she asked.

"Yup. And I'm going back right after lunch too."

"Wow," Elizabeth said, obviously impressed. "You're really working hard."

Jessica sighed. "You've got to work hard if you want to win." She squinted at Elizabeth. "Are you actually doing homework on this beautiful day?"

"Mmhmm." Elizabeth turned a page in her notebook. "I'm working on my essay for English class. Have you started yours yet?"

"No." Jessica shook her head. At the moment, she wasn't even sure what the assignment was. Something about choosing a phrase from Mr.

Bowman's list and writing five hundred words on whether you agreed or disagreed.

"I'm doing mine on 'An eye for an eye,'" Elizabeth said.

"Good topic." Jessica nodded her approval. After all, that was exactly what had happened with her and Dawn. Dawn had sabotaged her performance, so Jessica had sabotaged Dawn's back. An eye for an eye.

"I don't think an eye for an eye is fair and just punishment," Elizabeth said.

"You don't?" Jessica glanced at Elizabeth with surprise. "You mean if you poke my eye out, you don't think I should have the right to poke yours out? What else am I supposed to do?"

"Well, you *could* just walk away," Elizabeth suggested.

Jessica's nostrils flared. "Why should I?" she asked.

Elizabeth raised her eyebrows. "Jess, this is a hypothetical situation. I'm not saying *you* should do anything."

Jessica's back suddenly broke out in a sweat. "Well—I know that."

"Then how come you look so upset?" Elizabeth asked.

"Upset?" Jessica repeated weakly. "I'm not upset. I'm just—tired. Or hungry. Yeah, that's it. I'm hungry." She stood up. "I think I'll go get something to eat and then I better head back to the gym."

"Try one of those fig bars that Mom made," Elizabeth told her. "They're really yummy."

"OK," Jessica opened the sliding glass door and

dashed into the kitchen. But she didn't take a fig bar. Instead, she grabbed the phone book. One thing was certain. Not knowing what really happened to Dawn was making her crazy. She had to call the Weston coach, just to make sure everything was all right.

She's probably fine, Jessica told herself, flipping the pages. But she wanted to hear it for herself anyway. Once she did, she could get back to her regularly scheduled life.

SEVEN

"What did you say your name was?" Coach Wykoff asked.

Jessica cleared her throat. Actually, she hadn't given a name. "Uh, my name is Elizabeth. Elizabeth Fowler," she said, doodling on the cover of the phone book with her pencil. "I don't really know Dawn, but I'm a big fan and I saw her fall on Thursday and, well, I guess I was worried about her."

"We're all worried about her," Mr. Wykoff said. "What happened on Thursday was terribly unfortunate."

Jessica swallowed hard. "Terribly unfortunate?" she repeated, trying to keep her voice steady.

"Gymnasts get hurt," Mr. Wykoff went on. "It's part of the sport. But it's unfortunate when they get hurt so close to a competition like the California Games."

Jessica swallowed again. Dawn wasn't supposed

to get hurt! Jessica just wanted to, well, show Dawn what it was like to have someone sabotage your routine. *An eye for an eye.*

"Dawn *will* be able to compete in the Games, won't she?" Jessica asked worriedly.

"I don't know," the coach replied with a heavy sigh. "Her ankle is giving her a lot of trouble. She couldn't even practice yesterday."

"Couldn't practice?" Suddenly Jessica imagined Dawn lying in a hospital bed, her body writhing in pain.

"We told her to take the weekend off, just lie around with that ankle propped up and we'll see how she is on Monday."

I've destroyed her gymnastic career, Jessica realized with a shiver. *Maybe even her whole life! What if she never walks again?*

"D-d-do you know what happened on Thursday?" Jessica asked, chewing nervously on her pencil. Her heart was pounding like a sledgehammer.

"She just slipped," Mr. Wykoff replied. "It happens. Even to the best of gymnasts. Listen, would you like Dawn's phone number? She could probably tell you how she's doing better than I could. And I'm sure she'd appreciate your concern."

"Oh, I don't know," Jessica said. It was one thing to call up Dawn's coach, but calling Dawn directly was another story.

"Don't be nervous," Mr. Wykoff said. "She may be a terrific gymnast, but deep down, she's a regular kid just like you."

Jessica gave a short laugh. "I'm sure. Just like me."

Mr. Wycoff told her the number, and Jessica copied it down, just to get the coach off her back. But she had no intention of dialing it.

Donald stood at the edge of the mat with a copy of *How to Do Gymnastics* in his hand and stared down the runway at the vault. His book said the vault stood four feet high. He'd studied enough physics to know that the force generated from hitting the springboard should be enough to propel him up and over the vault, but still, when you are only four feet ten, you can't help but worry.

Donald reread the section in his book that compared vaulting to a game of leapfrog. He used to play leapfrog with his cousins. But it was one thing to leap over a hunched-down kid, who was maybe only a foot and a half off the ground, and quite another to leap over a four-foot-high block of wood and steel.

But Donald was determined to do it. He set the book down on the ground and took a deep breath. He was the only one in the gym. The others weren't due to arrive for a good half hour yet. So if he made an idiot of himself, there would be no one around to see him do it.

"Here goes nothing," Donald muttered. He ran down the mat toward the vault as fast as he could. But as he hit the springboard, he rammed his stomach into the front of the horse. The rest of his body continued over the horse and he landed in a heap on the mat below.

"Don't tell me," said a voice from the door. "It's another Donald Zwerdling Zzzpecial."

Donald rolled over onto his stomach and peered between the legs of the vault. Lila Fowler stood in the doorway.

"Oh man," Donald moaned as he dropped his head to the mat. "Not you! Anybody but you!"

"Funny," Lila said. "I was just thinking the exact same thing about *you*." Her shoes clicked on the floor as she went into the locker room across the hall.

Donald sighed. Was all this torture really worth it?

I should get back to the gym, Jessica told herself as she drank a glass of juice by the kitchen sink. But somehow, she couldn't pry her eyes away from the phone. And the piece of paper with Dawn's number scrawled on it.

I'll just give her a quick call to make sure things are OK, Jessica told herself. She went to the table and picked up the receiver. But after she punched in the first three numbers, she slammed the receiver down. *What should I say?* she wondered. *Hello, this is Jessica Wakefield and I'm just calling to see how badly I hurt you the other day?*

Jessica picked up her gym bag, determined to go to practice. But a voice inside her head stopped her. *You don't have to call her up as Jessica Wakefield. You told her coach your name was Elizabeth Fowler and you were just a concerned fan.*

The coach had given Elizabeth Fowler Dawn's phone number. He might even ask Dawn whether an Elizabeth Fowler had called her. Jessica set her gym bag down again. This would only take a minute.

She punched in the number and waited while the

phone rang once, twice, three times . . . "Hello!" barked a girl's angry voice.

Jessica cleared her throat. "Uh, I'd like to speak to Dawn, please."

"This is Dawn. Who's this?" the girl said frostily.

"My name is Elizabeth Fowler," Jessica said, her heart pounding. "I uh, got your number from your coach. I just wanted to see how you were, you know, after your fall on Thursday?"

"Well, I don't mind telling you I spent *five* hours in the emergency room Thursday night," Dawn said. "I have to be on crutches. I can't practice. And now—" She broke off as if the rest were too painful to talk about.

But Jessica had to know. "And now what?" she whispered, her hands shaking.

"I—I might not be able to go to the California Games!" Dawn exclaimed tearfully.

Jessica's stomach knotted. Dawn might have to miss the California Games—because of *her*?

"Listen," Jessica said hesitantly. "If there's anything I can do—"

"*Do!*" Dawn practically screamed. "There's nothing you can *do!* There's nothing *anybody* can do!"

And then she hung up.

OK, this is it, Donald told himself as he stared down the runway at the vault once again. *This time I'm really going to do it! I'm going to run down there, hit the springboard, and leapfrog over the vault!*

Most of the girls were warming up in small groups all around the gym. It wouldn't be long before they kicked him off the vault. *It's now or never.*

He took a deep breath. Then he ran down the runway as fast as he could. He hit the springboard exactly right and his entire body sprang up. But he forgot to put his hands down on the horse. He hit the horse with his knees and fell the rest of the way over.

"Boy, some people just don't know when to quit," Lila muttered as she got down on the floor to begin her stretches.

Mary Wallace touched her nose to her knee. "Well, you've got to admire his persistence," she said.

Lila tossed her long brown hair. "I don't have to admire *anything* about Donald Zwerdling."

"What are you doing?" Elizabeth asked.

Jessica jumped. "You scared me to death!" she said, glancing at her sister with annoyance.

"Sorry." Elizabeth examined the bandages, food, and music Jessica had assembled on the kitchen table. "But what *is* all this stuff for?"

"One of the gymnasts got hurt the other day," Jessica replied as she lined the bottom of a wicker basket with a pretty pink towel. "So I'm making up a little care package for her."

Elizabeth picked up the Johnny Buck CD. "This looks helpful," she remarked. "She'll be as good as new after she listens to this."

Jessica snatched the CD out of Elizabeth's hand and tossed it in the basket. "It's to take her mind off her pain."

"Oh." Elizabeth bit into an apple. "So who got hurt?"

"Uh, nobody you know," Jessica replied, quickly filling the basket with a bunch of grapes, a Snapple, the latest *Teen Dream* magazine, and an Ace bandage. "I'm going to drop this off on my way to practice," she said as she picked up her gym bag. "I'll see you later!"

Why am I doing this? Jessica asked herself as she pedaled up another hill. Her basket of goodies was hooked over one side of her handlebars. Her gym bag was hooked over the other.

Because it's a nice thing to do.

She figured she'd just set the basket on Dawn's front porch and leave. No one would know who had dropped it off. Dawn certainly wouldn't think it came from Jessica Wakefield.

Jessica checked her watch. It was 1:15. This was taking longer than she thought it would.

Finally she entered Dawn's neighborhood. It wasn't as nice as her own. The trees were taller, but they hid cracked sidewalks and unkempt lawns.

Jessica found the address she was looking for. A small yellow house with peeling paint. Someone was sitting in an old flowery lounge chair on the rickety front porch—someone with dark curly hair and a bandaged foot. Jessica drew in her breath. It was *Dawn!*

Now what? Jessica wondered as she stopped near the front walk. She hadn't expected Dawn to be sitting outside.

Dawn glanced at her with annoyance. "What are *you* doing here?" she asked.

Jessica bit her lip. She considered turning her bike around and pedaling away as fast as she could. But what would be the point? Dawn had already seen her. She might as well do what she came to do.

She nudged her kickstand down with her foot and took a deep breath. "I uh, brought you something," she said as she headed up the walk.

Dawn glanced at the basket with mild interest, then narrowed her eyes. "What for? Are you feeling guilty for what you did to me?"

"Guilty?" Jessica repeated as though she'd never heard the word before. "Why should I feel guilty?"

Dawn shrugged. "I don't know exactly what you did, but I know you messed up my bars routine somehow." She turned a page in her magazine.

Jessica's mouth dropped open. "Well, I-I-I only did it because you messed up my routine first!" she stammered.

"I did not!" Dawn shook her head.

"What do you call putting oil on the bars right before my performance?" Jessica asked, hands on her hips.

"I don't know what you're talking about," Dawn said, forcefully turning another page in her magazine.

"You know exactly what I'm talking about!" Jessica cried, outraged. "You sabotaged me and I sabotaged you. At least I have the guts to come over here!"

"I don't have to listen to your irrational accusations!" Dawn screamed as she flung her magazine down. "Go away, Jessica." She stood up and hobbled inside. She slammed the door shut behind her.

Jessica stared dumbfounded at the closed door. *That girl has a serious attitude problem,* she thought. She set the basket down, then turned around and headed for her bike. She was through worrying about Dawn Maven. Now it was time to concentrate on gymnastics.

EIGHT

"Where have you been, Jessica?" Lila asked, hands on her hips as Jessica dashed into the gym. "Practice began forty-five minutes ago, you know."

"Yeah, I know. But I, uh, had something to do," Jessica replied, sitting down on the floor to begin her stretches.

She finished her warm-ups and went over to wait her turn at the uneven parallel bars. Mary was spotting Brooke Dennis. They both looked more serious than Jessica had ever seen them.

Everybody seemed serious today, Jessica noted as she put on her grips. There was a lot less chattering going on. People were either practicing or waiting for a turn to practice. And for once Donald Zwerdling was just sitting on the bench watching instead of getting in everyone's way.

The California Games were only a week away.

There were no meets scheduled this week, only practices. And there were practices scheduled every day.

Brooke finished her routine with a straddle sole circle dismount. "Your turn, Jessica," she said.

Jessica nodded as she chalked her hands, then headed over to the bars. But as she was about to jump up to the high bar, images of Dawn suddenly flashed through her mind. Dawn crashing to the ground. Dawn holding her leg and screaming in agony. Dawn sitting on the lounge chair at her house, her foot bandaged.

Jessica drew in her breath. *Gymnasts get hurt.* That was what Dawn's coach had said. *It's unfortunate when they get hurt so close to a performance.*

What if I get hurt right before the California Games? Jessica thought, a chill going up her spine.

"Jessica! Are you just going to stand there or are you going to practice?" Lila demanded from a few feet away.

"I'm going to practice!" Jessica snapped. She pushed her scary thoughts away and jumped up to the high bar.

But as she dropped her eyes to the mat below, she remembered how Dawn had lain there, screaming, "My leg! My leg!"

Jessica immediately jumped down. Her whole body was shaking.

"Come *on,* Jessica!" Lila said impatiently. "The rest of us would like to use the bars too!"

"So, go ahead and use them," Jessica said, nodding toward the bars as she stepped off the thick mat. "You probably need the practice more than I do anyway."

Coach Arlin walked briskly over to where the girls were standing. "You were up there first, Jessica," she said. "I want to see how that double flyaway is coming along."

Lila rolled her eyes and sat down on the floor.

"It's coming along fine." Jessica shrugged. "I don't mind if Lila uses the bars now."

"First, I'd like to see your double flyaway." Coach Arlin pointed toward the apparatus.

Jessica sighed. Obviously Coach Arlin was in one of her insistent moods. "All right," she said grudgingly. She went to rechalk her grips.

"Why don't you run through your whole routine while you're up there," Coach Arlin said.

"Sure," Jessica responded. She smiled weakly at her coach as she walked over to the bars.

She mounted the low bar and began her routine.

Gymnasts get hurt. Dawn's coach's words echoed inside her head.

Stop it! Jessica told herself.

She squatted on the low bar and leaped to the high bar. But she didn't swing high enough to reach her handstand. She dropped her eyes to the floor. *Boy, it's a long way down there,* she thought breathlessly as she swung back and forth. Suddenly she let go of the bar. Her body hit the mat with a thud.

That's it. Now I can't go to the California Games either, Jessica thought miserably.

But as she sat up and tested her arms and legs she realized she wasn't hurt.

"Get back up there and try it again," Coach Arlin said gently.

Jessica shook her head. "I don't think so." She rose slowly to her feet. "I uh, have a feeling today just isn't my day for the uneven bars."

"You sure are acting weird today, Jessica," Lila remarked.

"It almost looks like you're scared," Coach Arlin observed.

"Scared?" Jessica cried. "Me?" She pointed to her chest and laughed. "It's just that, well, I've been spending so much time on this routine that I'm getting nervous about my other events." She glanced desperately around the gym for an open apparatus. Amy Sutton was just finishing up on the floor. *Perfect!*

"I think I should practice my floor exercise. OK?" She glanced at her coach. "I promise I'll come back and do the bars later."

Coach Arlin frowned. "When you develop a sudden fear like this, you should face it head on."

"I'm not afraid!" Jessica insisted loudly.

Coach Arlin sighed. "All right. Go ahead and run through your floor exercise. But I want to see you back on the bars *today*."

Jessica nodded. "You will," she promised. But deep down she wasn't so sure.

Elizabeth peeked through Jessica's door at eleven o'clock on Sunday morning. She knew that her twin liked to sleep in, but this was a little ridiculous.

The blinds were still drawn, but as Elizabeth approached the bed, she could see that Jessica's eyes were open. "Oh good," she said. "You *are* awake."

Jessica yawned and stretched. "Yeah, I'm awake," she said. "What's up?"

"I want to interview you for the *Sixers*," Elizabeth said with a smile.

Jessica's forehead wrinkled. "The *Sixers?*"

Elizabeth nodded enthusiastically. "Just like you've always wanted."

Jessica yawned once more and sat up slowly. "All right, I guess."

Elizabeth frowned. *Maybe she's still tired,* she thought. After all, Jessica spent practically every waking moment at the gym these days.

Elizabeth plopped down on the bed next to Jess and opened her notebook. "Well, let's get started. Why don't you tell me what it's like being on the Sweet Valley gymnastics team?" She held her pencil poised over her paper, ready to copy down every word Jessica said.

"It's OK." Jessica shrugged.

Elizabeth stared at her sister in disbelief. "It's *OK?* Jess, you're going to the California Games and all you can say about it is 'it's OK?'"

Jessica picked a fuzz ball off her blanket. "I guess we're so busy getting ready for the Games that I haven't had much time to think about it."

Elizabeth touched her sister's arm. "What's the matter, Jess? Are all these extra practices getting to you?"

Jessica shook her head and nibbled on her pinkie.

Well, something's bothering her, Elizabeth thought. Jessica wouldn't normally ruin her nail polish by biting her nails.

"Is it that girl from Weston?" Elizabeth asked. "Are you upset about what happened to her?"

Jessica's eyes flashed. "How did you know about that?" she demanded.

Elizabeth smiled. Now she was getting somewhere. "I was at the meet. I saw her fall. She's your biggest competition, isn't she?" she said sympathetically.

Jessica nodded without looking Elizabeth in the eye.

"Well, I can see why you're upset," Elizabeth said. "I mean, if you win the gold, but you don't get to compete against that girl, you'll probably always wonder whether you would've beaten her. You'll never know whether you really deserved the medal or not."

Jessica looked up with surprise. "I won't?"

"Well, that's assuming you *do* win the gold, of course." Elizabeth laughed. "But people say you're the favorite."

Jessica smiled faintly as she dropped her eyes again.

"Cheer up, Jess," Elizabeth said. "That girl is going to have to heal on her own. There isn't anything you can do for her. You just have to concentrate on your own routines."

Jessica nodded and sighed deeply. "You're right, Elizabeth," she said.

Elizabeth smiled. "So why don't you tell me about your routines?" she asked as she adjusted the notebook in her lap.

Jessica lay back against her pillows, fingering her blanket. Elizabeth had finished her interview and gone back to her room, but Jessica couldn't stop thinking about what she had said.

Elizabeth was right. What good was a gold medal at the California Games if Jessica didn't get to face her stiffest competition? She really did want to compete against Dawn. She wanted to compete against her fair and square.

Elizabeth had also said there was nothing she could do about Dawn. But maybe there was. Jessica suddenly sat up in bed. Maybe she could go over to Weston and help Dawn get back in shape . . . help her train.

Not because she was feeling guilty. No, she just wanted to make sure Dawn would compete at the California Games. That way, Jessica would have the chance to beat her and prove to everyone she really was the *best!*

Jessica smiled at her reflection in the mirror. She was feeling much better now. She'd cut out of practice a little early tomorrow afternoon and bike over to Weston Middle School.

"Can I have just two minutes?" Donald Zwerdling begged Jessica just as she was about to climb on the balance beam.

Before Jessica could answer, he hopped up onto the beam. Jessica had to cover her smile as she watched him take two steps, then hop up about two inches above the beam. "Hey, I did it!" he said, glancing around the gym at anyone who might be paying attention.

No one else was.

Donald took two more steps and did another little hop. He was gaining confidence now. "OK, here comes my big Donald Zwerdling Zzzpecial!" he said as he ran down the length of the beam.

Jessica wasn't sure what exactly the Donald Zwerdling Zzzpecial was supposed to be this time, but Donald leaped up into the air when he reached the edge of the beam. As he came down, he grabbed at the air and took one, two, three, four, five giant steps, spinning out of control toward the uneven parallel bars.

Jessica gasped as she watched Donald crash into Lila, who was hanging from the top bar. They both fell to the ground.

"Donald!" Lila screamed, punching the mat with her fists.

"Uh, sorry," Donald replied as he rubbed his leg.

Jessica ran over to them. "Are you guys OK?"

Lila glared at Donald as Jessica helped her to her feet. "He could've killed me!" she cried. "Did you see that?" Lila turned to Ms. Arlin, who had joined them under the bars. "He came barreling over here like a maniac and knocked me down right in the middle of my routine!"

"Donald, you really have to be more careful," Coach Arlin told him sternly.

He hung his head in shame. "I will, Coach Arlin. I'm really sorry, Lila."

"Yeah, well, sorry doesn't help much if I've got a broken hip, now, does it?" Lila spat out, rubbing her right hip.

"Actually, I think you fell on your butt, not your hip," Donald said with a smirk.

Lila's mouth dropped open in horror. She crossed

her arms and narrowed her eyes. "You wouldn't know your butt from your elbow!" she barked.

"OK, that's enough!" Coach Arlin said sternly. "It's time to get back to work."

"Do you want to run through your routine on the bars?" Lila asked. "I'll spot you."

Jessica shook her head. She felt numb. What happened to Lila *could've* happened to her. "I think I'll run through my beam routine and then I'm going to head out. It's been a rough day."

"Tell me about it," Lila said as she jumped up to the high bar to begin her routine again. "I'll catch up with you in the locker room."

Jessica nodded. She took a deep breath and headed over to the beam. But there were three people ahead of her. She glanced up at the clock. It was already four-thirty. Maybe she'd just blow off the rest of practice. She really wasn't in the mood for it, anyway. And she wanted to make sure she didn't miss Dawn. It would take a while to bike over to Weston and she didn't know how long the Weston team practiced.

Jessica glanced over her shoulder at Lila once more. She was amazed at how Lila spun up and over the high bar as though nothing had happened. She wasn't at all afraid. Not that Jessica was exactly afraid either. No, what Jessica was experiencing was a sympathetic reaction. *Yeah, that's it,* she told herself. *As long as Dawn can't perform, I can't either.*

Jessica had to get Dawn back on her feet. And then she'd give Dawn the competition of her life.

NINE

"Hey, Jessica, where are you going?"

Jessica turned around reluctantly. She had hoped to sneak out before anybody noticed, but Lila had caught her in the hallway. "I've, uh, got things to do," she replied.

Lila wrinkled her nose. "What things?"

"Just things," Jessica replied as she headed for the door. "I'll see you tomorrow."

"Wait!" Lila grabbed Jessica's arm. "I'm calling an emergency Unicorn Club meeting after practice today."

"What for?" Jessica asked.

"To see what we can do to get Donald Zwerdling out of our gym permanently!"

"Oh, come on, Lila," Jessica said, glancing at her watch. There was no way she could squeeze in a Unicorn meeting today. "You didn't get hurt that badly. Just let Ms. Arlin deal with him."

"But she's *not* dealing with him," Lila protested. "That's the point. You were there, Jessica. You saw what happened. I'm counting on you to be at this meeting and tell everybody exactly what you saw!"

"Well, I'm sorry, Lila," Jessica said as she started down the hall again. "But I—have things to do."

"Hey!" Lila yelled. Her voice echoed down the corridor. "Where are you going that's so important?"

But Jessica walked as fast as she could to the door, as though she didn't even hear.

Jessica approached the main entrance of Weston Middle School with an uneasy feeling in her stomach. She hadn't noticed how old the building and neighborhood were when she was at Weston for the meet. The red bricks on the outside were faded and crumbling. There were patches of dead grass throughout the lawn, and there was dirt where the grass had worn away altogether. But what really surprised Jessica was the *metal detector* she discovered when she pulled open the heavy brown door to the building.

She entered the building and crept down a flight of stairs to the gymnasium, where they'd had their meet. Peering into the gym, she saw Dawn sitting with her arms crossed on a bench against the far wall. She was wearing jeans and a button-down shirt. Her brown hair fell loose and curly just below her shoulders. Jessica couldn't tell whether her ankle was still wrapped or not.

Jessica stepped away from the door and leaned against the cool brick wall. She didn't *have* to go in.

She could go back outside, get on her bike, and go home. No one would ever know she was here.

No. She'd cut out of her own practice early and biked all the way up here. She wasn't going to back out now. She was going to get Dawn ready for competition.

Even if it costs you the gold medal? a small voice inside her whispered.

But it *wouldn't* cost her the gold, Jessica assured herself. Dawn was good, but she was better.

Jessica took a deep breath and walked into the gym. Most of the girls were too busy practicing or watching teammates practicing to notice Jessica. But Dawn's eyebrows rose in surprise when Jessica walked in. With her jaw set tight, she immediately got up and stomped toward Jessica with only a slight limp.

"Hey, you're walking much better today," Jessica said cheerfully.

"Never mind that," Dawn said, crossing her arms and glaring up at Jessica, who was half a head taller. "What are you doing here?"

Jessica frowned. After she'd biked all the way over here Dawn could at least be nice. "Why don't we sit down—"

"I don't want to sit down with *you!*" Dawn interrupted. Her eyes flashed with anger. "Why don't you just say what you came to say and then get out of here!"

Jessica's face burned. "Do you always have to be so nasty?" she snapped. "For your information, I'm here to help you get back into shape!"

Dawn snorted. "Oh sure. First you practically break my ankle—"

"Hey!" Jessica stopped her. "You sabotaged me first! And don't you forget it!"

"Why don't you just leave?" Dawn said as she turned away.

"No! I want to help you—"

"I don't want your help!"

"Hey, Dawn!" Coach Wykoff came toward them. Jessica drew in her breath. She hadn't noticed how cute he was before. He was tall and tan with wavy blond hair and a gorgeous smile. "Who's your friend?"

"She's *not* my friend!" Dawn barked.

Coach Wykoff tapped his chin thoughtfully. "Don't tell me. Elizabeth Fowler, right?"

Dawn's forehead wrinkled in confusion as she glanced at Jessica.

Jessica didn't know what to say. Didn't the coach recognize her as the star of the Sweet Valley gymnastics team? Maybe not. She wasn't wearing her leotard and her hair wasn't tied back.

"I'm glad you came over today," Coach Wykoff said, placing a hand on Jessica's shoulder. "Dawn could use a friend."

Dawn snickered.

Coach Wykoff smiled again, then went to talk to the girl on the beam.

Dawn glanced sideways at Jessica. "*You're* Elizabeth Fowler?" she asked with disbelief.

Jessica looked away. "Yeah," she said with a sigh.

Dawn snorted. "I should have guessed. Elizabeth is your twin sister and there's a somebody Fowler on your team."

Jessica couldn't help smiling. "Wow. You really did some research on me!"

Dawn glared at Jessica. "I also know you have an ego the size of California," she said.

Jessica's mouth dropped open. This girl was really some piece of work! "Well, if mine's the size of California, yours must be the size of the whole world," she retorted.

Dawn crossed her arms. "Well, if that's the way you feel, why don't you just leave now!"

Jessica gritted her teeth. In a way there was nothing she'd like better than to leave the Weston gym for good. But she wasn't about to let Dawn have her way so easily. With a toss of her head, she stalked over to the bench and sat down. She wasn't going anywhere.

"So why do you want to help me so much anyway?"

Jessica looked up a few minutes later to see Dawn standing right in front of her. "Because I want to compete against you fair and square at the California Games," Jessica said simply. "When I win the gold, I want to know I really am the best. And I won't know that if I can't compete against you."

"Aw, isn't that sweet!" Dawn rolled her eyes as she sank down onto the bench.

"Well, there's obviously no point in actually *talking* to you." Jessica stood up and grabbed her backpack. "But whether you like it or not, I will be back. I'll come every day after my own practice. We'll get you back in shape."

Dawn pressed her lips together tightly. She stared

straight ahead as though she hadn't even heard Jessica.

"See you tomorrow," Jessica told her.

OK, no more excuses, Jessica told herself at practice the next day. She was going to get back on those uneven parallel bars.

She mounted the low bar and began her routine. But it was the same as last week. Images of Dawn's fall filled her head.

Keep going! she ordered herself. Up and over, back and around. It wasn't so bad on the low bar. Her heart was pounding, but she was doing it. Once she switched back to the high bar, though, she choked. *Gymnasts get hurt!* In a panic, she jumped down.

She stared at the bars in front of her, breathing raggedly. What was her problem? Jessica Wakefield had never been afraid of anything before.

She jumped back up and tried again. She decided to forget about her routine for now and just concentrate on the moves—especially the high bar moves.

She swung back and forth, higher and higher, getting ready to go into a giant swing and then do her double flyaway dismount. But once she got up there, she choked again. Instead of swinging up and over the high bar, she dropped her elbows, caught her foot on the low bar and fell to the mat below.

Coach Arlin rushed toward Jessica. "Are you OK?" she asked worriedly.

"I'm—fine," Jessica replied weakly.

Coach Arlin helped her to her feet. "You know, Jessica, it's not uncommon for gymnasts to develop a sudden fear—"

"I'm not afraid!" Jessica said for what felt like the millionth time.

"Well, why don't you stay a few minutes late tonight and we'll see if we can't work through whatever's troubling you," Ms. Arlin said. "OK?"

"Nothing's troubling me," Jessica insisted. "Besides, I have plans right after practice. In fact, I should probably leave early."

Coach Arlin frowned. "I wish you wouldn't. I'd like to have some one-on-one time with you."

"But I don't need it," Jessica told her firmly. She straightened her spine so that she looked tall and graceful, then glanced at the clock on the wall. "Look, I should probably go now."

"But Jessica—"

"See you later!" Jessica called over her shoulder as she marched toward the door. She couldn't wait to get out of the gym, away from the bars and from her coach's questioning eyes.

So, she really did come, Dawn Maven thought as she watched Jessica Wakefield enter Weston's gym. Dawn was the only one still practicing. The others had all gone home.

Dawn turned her back to Jessica and hopped up to the high bar. She didn't want Jessica to think she'd actually been waiting for her. She didn't need Jessica Wakefield's help. She didn't need *anyone's* help!

"You're dressed for practice today," Jessica commented. "Good!"

"Of course I'm dressed," Dawn replied, hanging

upside down. "Did you think I'd come to the gym naked?"

"Here we go again," Jessica sighed as she hugged the cables at the side of the apparatus. "Do you always have to be so sarcastic?"

"If you don't like it, you can leave," Dawn retorted.

"I'm not leaving," Jessica said stubbornly. "By the way, your legs weren't together on that last turn."

"Who asked you?" Dawn snapped as she dipped and swung again. This time she made sure to keep her legs together.

"That's better." Jessica nodded. She bent down to tie her shoe and a curtain of hair fell over her face.

Dawn let her body hang until her swings slowed. Then she carefully let go of the bar.

"What was that?" Jessica asked, raising her head. "Why didn't you do a regular dismount?"

Dawn sighed. "If it's all the same to you, I'd just as soon not stress my ankle by coming down hard on it."

"Well, fine!" Jessica said, planting a hand on her hip.

"Fine!" Dawn repeated.

"Why don't you get back up there?" Jessica asked, flipping her hair over her shoulder. "I want to talk to you about your pirouette next."

"*Next?*" Dawn clucked her tongue. "Who do you think you are, my coach?" She knew that her pirouette needed work, but who was Jessica to give her pointers?

Jessica folded her arms. "You need to move your first hand down the bar."

Dawn bit her lip. Her coach had been telling her the same thing for weeks.

"Get up there and try it," Jessica insisted.

"Oh, all right," Dawn grumbled. She'd do it because she knew she needed the practice, not because Jessica Wakefield told her to. She hopped up to the high bar and casted to a handstand.

"Point your toes," Jessica said, just as Dawn was about to change her hands.

Dawn sighed as she swung around the bar again. "For your information, my toes are a lot more pointed in competition than yours are!"

"Yeah, well, they weren't very pointed two minutes ago," Jessica informed her.

"That's because you're bugging me! Would you please shut up so I can do this?" she yelled.

Jessica pantomimed zipping her lip.

Dawn rolled her eyes. Once she was sure Jessica would keep her mouth shut for ten seconds, she went into her pirouette. As soon as she got into a handstand on the high bar, she released her hand and turned it around and—"Argh!" she cried. There wasn't time to move down the bar. She had to turn the rest of her body *now* or risk falling.

"You're still not moving your hand," Jessica said.

"I know that!" Dawn exclaimed. She let her body slow, then let herself down onto her good foot.

She flexed her fingers and stretched her shoulders. Then she went to dust her hands with chalk again.

"If you tune into your body, you'll find out there's like a two-second window when you're totally balanced on top of the bar," Jessica told her. "*That's* when you start the changeover. Not one second before."

Dawn glared at her, but didn't say anything. She knew exactly what she had to do. The problem was actually doing it.

She jumped up to the high bar, swung back and forth, and tried the move again. Same thing. She didn't move her hand. "Don't even say it!" she barked at Jessica.

She allowed her body to keep swinging. And when she felt ready, she tried the move one more time. But this time she nearly missed the bar completely when she attempted the changeover. "I'm never going to get this!" she cried as she dropped to the mat.

"Yes, you will," Jessica said softly, pulling out two Snapple iced teas from the purple gym bag at her feet. She held one out to Dawn.

Dawn shook her head. She didn't have any money on her and the last thing she wanted was to be indebted to Jessica Wakefield.

"Oh come on," Jessica said with annoyance. "Even my Snapple isn't good enough for you?"

Dawn rolled her eyes. "Fine, I'll take it," she said holding out her hand. After all, she *was* thirsty. "Thanks," she said under her breath.

Dawn unscrewed the cap and took a sip, aware of Jessica's eyes on her the whole time. "What?" she asked. "Why are you looking at me like that?"

Jessica took a deep breath. "Dawn? Do you ever get scared when you're up there?"

Dawn stared disbelievingly at Jessica. "No way!"

Jessica turned away. "I didn't think so," she said softly.

But as Dawn took another sip, she wondered

whether Jessica noticed she was trembling. Just hearing Jessica's question out loud started Dawn's pulse racing.

Fear. It was something that could destroy a gymnast's career.

Beware of fear, her coach always said. *Fear is your greatest enemy.* Any time a gymnast fell in his gym, he made her get right back up and do the move again. But that was never a problem for Dawn. Dawn wasn't afraid of *falling*. She was afraid of failing.

TEN

"Jessica!" Lila called.

It was Wednesday morning, and Jessica was on her way to her third-period class. "Hi, Lila," she said, stopping to wait for her friend.

But Lila wasn't looking very friendly this morning. "My chauffeur saw you on the corner of Spruce and Forty-second Avenue last night," she said in an accusatory voice.

Jessica swallowed hard. Where was Forty-second? Was that the address of Weston Middle School?

"He said you were on your *bike!*" Lila went on.

"Uh, was he sure it was me?" Jessica asked weakly. This was all she needed. Someone finding out about her trips to the Weston gym. "Lots of girls look like me."

Lila shook her head. "Only *one* girl looks like you. And that's Elizabeth. But it couldn't have been

Elizabeth. My chauffeur said the girl he saw was carrying a purple gym bag."

"Oh," Jessica said as she and Lila started walking again. *Quick. Make something up,* Jessica told herself. *Some legitimate reason for biking over there.*

"I don't know what you're doing taking a long bike ride like that," Lila continued. "The California Games are *this* Saturday! You should be saving your energy."

Saving my energy? Jessica felt a wave of relief. Lila wasn't concerned about where Jessica had gone, she was concerned that Jessica had taken too long of a bike ride. "Well, I was just trying to get into shape for the Games—you know, strengthening my leg muscles." She jogged a few steps, bringing her knees close to her chest, to show Lila just how strong she was.

Lila smiled. "Yeah, well, maybe next time you should bike in the other direction. Do you have any idea how close to Weston Middle School you were?"

"Uh, pretty close, I guess," Jessica said sheepishly.

Lila nodded. "Next time, bike in the other direction," she repeated. Then she disappeared around the corner.

"Come on, Donald," Lila said with annoyance. "Ms. Arlin said we get priority on all the equipment. And right now, I want to practice my vault."

"Just give me one more chance," Donald pleaded. He was on a roll. He had gotten over the vault the last time. But he'd caught his foot on the way over, so he didn't actually land it. "I promise, whether I make it or not, you get the next turn."

Lila rolled her eyes. "Like you'll really make it," she muttered. "All right, Donald. I'm feeling generous today. I'll give you one chance. But one chance *only*." She held up her index finger. "And make it quick. I haven't got all day."

Donald stared down the length of the runway. He could almost hear the music from that great sports movie *Chariots of Fire* playing in his head. He pictured himself running down the mat in slow motion, in rhythm with the song, and then leaping over the vault and sticking the landing.

"Are you planning to do this sometime today, Donald?" Lila asked. She stood with her arms crossed, tapping her foot.

"I'm going to do it right now," Donald replied with determination.

He sprinted down the mat, pounced on the springboard, leapfrogged over the vault, and landed hard on his feet just like he'd imagined.

Donald stared at his feet in disbelief. Then he turned to Lila. "I did it," he whispered. "Did you see that?"

Donald couldn't help noticing that Lila didn't look especially impressed, but at that moment he didn't care.

"*I did it! I did it! I did it!*" he cried as he chicken danced around the mat.

"What did you do?" Amy asked from the beam.

Donald turned. He'd attracted the attention of every girl in the gym. That was almost more exciting than the fact he'd landed a vault. *Almost,* but not quite. "I landed my Donald Zwerdling

Zzzpecial!" he announced to anyone who would listen.

Lila pretended to yawn. "He landed a squat vault. Big deal."

"All right, Donald!" Amy cheered.

"It's a start," Mary added.

They were all applauding for him. Even Jessica and Coach Arlin. The only one who wasn't applauding was Lila. "Could we get back to our regularly scheduled practice now?" she asked.

"Oh come on, Lila," Mary said. "Don't you remember the first time you landed a vault?"

Lila looked blank. "No." She sniffed. "I probably landed it the first time I attempted it."

"Well, *I* think it's terrific," Coach Arlin said. "Good for you, Donald. You've really been working hard these last couple weeks."

Donald beamed. "I bet you guys wish you'd let me on your team now, don't you?"

"Yeah, right." Lila rolled her eyes.

Melissa raised an eyebrow, then turned back to her floor routine.

"That's OK." Donald shifted his weight from his toes to his heels. "I can see you need a towel boy more than you need another gymnast."

Coach Arlin smiled at him, then turned her attention to Jessica. "Should we run through your bars routine now?" she asked.

"Not right now." Jessica shook her head. "I've been waiting for a turn on the beam all day and I'm finally up next."

Donald scratched his head. Why was Jessica so

excited about the beam? The bars were her forte. It was her bars routine that had gotten the team to the California Games in the first place. But he couldn't remember the last time he'd seen Jessica on the bars. How was she going to perform her bars routine if she never practiced it?

Donald was beginning to feel like a part of the team. He'd been practicing with them and getting their towels and running errands for a couple of weeks now, after all. So maybe he wouldn't be totally out of line if he went to talk to Jessica.

He headed over to the beam.

"Hey Jessica!" Donald yelled as Jessica was just coming out of her English handstand-back walkover combination on the beam. "It's time to practice your bars routine."

Jessica shot him an irritated glance. "Can't you see I'm practicing my *beam* routine?" Who did he think he was, telling her what to do anyway?

She turned three cartwheels down the length of the beam, then spun around on her toes. But the spin was wobbly. That ape, Donald Zwerdling, was swinging his leg up over the beam!

"What are you *doing!*" Jessica cried, flinging her arms out to steady herself.

Donald grinned as he walked carefully toward her with his hands airplaned out to the sides. "I've come to personally escort you back to the bars," he announced with a low bow.

"Well thanks, but no thanks," she said. "Now *move!* I'm trying to practice here."

Donald crossed his arms and shook his head. "I'm not moving until you agree to get back on the bars," he said stubbornly.

"Oh yeah?" Jessica cocked her head. "We'll see about that." She grabbed his crossed arms and gave him a little shove.

"Whoa!" Donald cried, teetering from side to side until he managed to regain his balance.

Jessica gave him another shove.

"Jessica!" Coach Arlin cried with shock.

Jessica watched as Donald dropped down to the mat and landed on his feet. "It's OK, Ms. Arlin." Donald waved his hand dismissively. "She was up there first and I got in her way. But I only did it to get her to go back to the uneven parallel bars. She doesn't need practice on the beam. She needs practice on the bars."

"Thank you, Coach Zwerdling," Jessica said, rolling her eyes.

"Donald's right, Jessica," Ms. Arlin said. "Every time I ask you about your bars routine, you say, 'Later.' But later never comes."

"Yeah," Lila put in. "What are you so afraid of?"

Great, Jessica thought. The whole gym was watching her now.

"I'm not afraid!" Jessica told them all. Why were they all ganging up on her like this?

"Then prove it," Donald challenged her.

Jessica narrowed her eyes. "I don't have to prove anything to *you.*"

"Of course you don't," Donald replied. "But why not prove it to yourself? That's what I did. I proved to myself that I could land a Donald Zwerdling Zzzpecial. Now it's your turn to prove to yourself that you're just as good on the bars as you ever were."

"Come on, Jessica," Mary said. "We'd all like to see your uneven bars routine."

Jessica chewed her lip. She wanted to tell everyone to just leave her alone, but somehow she couldn't. She knew she had to get back up on the bars sometime. The California Games were in three days. *But what if I fall?*

"Jess-ica! Jess-ica!" Donald began the chant and soon Mary, Amy, and the others raised their right arms and joined in. "Jess-ica! Jess-ica! Jess-ica!"

"We're going to keep this up until you do your routine," Donald informed her. "Jess-ica! Jess-ica! Jess-ica!"

Jessica sighed. "Oh, all right," she said. "If you guys will leave me alone afterward." She jumped down from the beam and Donald held out his arm to her.

"Won't you let me escort you, Miss?" Donald asked, lifting his chin.

"Oh, give me a break!" Jessica rolled her eyes.

Donald wiggled his eyebrows, then nodded toward his outstretched elbow.

Jessica let out her breath. "Fine. Whatever," she said, taking his elbow and allowing herself to be escorted to the uneven parallel bars as though she were going to a ball.

"You can do it, Jessica," Coach Arlin said.

"Think serene thoughts," Amy said, handing her a pair of hand grips.

Jessica's heart was pounding as she put them

on. *Serene thoughts.* She chalked her grips and took a deep breath. *I can do it,* she repeated to herself. Then she mounted the low bar and began her routine.

She did a perfect handstand, then a glide kip, and a squat to stand on the low bar.

Maybe this isn't my best performance, Jessica thought as leaped to the high bar and then came back in a blind back-straddle. *Maybe my legs aren't perfectly straight and my toes aren't perfectly pointed. But at least I'm doing it.*

When she got to the handstand and pirouette, she thought of Dawn. Jessica had never had trouble with the hand change the way Dawn did. And she didn't have trouble today either. She moved smoothly from the pirouette to her next move.

"You're doing fine, Jessica," Coach Arlin said encouragingly.

She was almost done now. Just the giant swing and her double flyaway dismount, which she landed perfectly.

She raised her hands to signal the end of her routine and then smiled at her teammates.

"All right, Jessica!" Amy clapped.

"Yay! Hooray!" Mary and Lila cheered.

Jessica fanned herself. "I told you I wasn't scared," she said coolly. *There. This proves it. I'm still a star.*

"Between Donald's vault and Jessica getting back up on the bars, I'd say we've had a pretty awesome practice today," Amy declared.

"I think this calls for a celebration," Coach

Arlin said. "How about we all go out for pizza after practice?"

"Yeah!" Amy nodded.

"Great!" Donald exclaimed.

Jessica's smile froze. "You don't mean *right* after practice, do you?" she asked.

"Well, that's what I was thinking," Coach Arlin replied. "I know how hungry you all get after practice."

"Well, um, I've got plans right after practice. Couldn't we do it in an hour or two?" Jessica asked.

"In an hour or two, the thrill of the moment will be gone," Lila protested. She grabbed Jessica's hand and stuck out her bottom lip in a pout. "You've run off somewhere after practice every single day this week. You can go out and have a little fun tonight."

"Yeah, you deserve it," Amy agreed.

Jessica fidgeted with her grips. She *had* to go to Weston. She had to get Dawn into shape so she could compete against her fair and square this Saturday.

Why? asked a voice inside her head. *It's not like she even appreciates you being there. She's always so nasty.*

"Come on, Jessica," Mary pressed. "This celebration is sort of for *you*. For getting back on the bars."

"I don't know." Jessica bit her lip.

Donald grabbed Jessica's arm from behind her back. "Do we have to twist your arm?" he asked.

Jessica smiled. Would it be so bad to skip Dawn's practice just this once? She could even stay a little later tomorrow to make up for it.

"OK," Jessica gave in finally. "I'll go." After all, Dawn probably wouldn't even miss her.

ELEVEN

"What are *you* doing here?" Dawn asked through gritted teeth as Jessica entered the Weston Middle School gym. Once again, Dawn was the only Weston gymnast still practicing.

Jessica walked around to the other side of the bars so she could see Dawn. But Dawn jumped down and turned away. She was heading for the drinking fountain on the other side of the gym.

"I told you I'd be here," Jessica said, trailing behind her.

"Yeah, you said you'd be here yesterday too," Dawn snapped.

Jessica smiled. "Gee, Dawn. I didn't know you cared."

Dawn stopped in her tracks. "I don't!" she spat over her shoulder. "Just go home, would you?" she barked. "I don't need you here."

Jessica watched as Dawn took a sip of water. Why did Dawn have to give her a guilt trip for not showing up yesterday? Not that she actually felt guilty, of course. She was here now. She wasn't going to leave.

She followed Dawn back to the uneven parallel bars. "How's your pirouette coming?" she asked, leaning against the side bar as Dawn put on her grips.

Dawn glared at her. "It's fine," she said through clenched teeth. "In fact, it's wonderful. If you'd been here yesterday you would have seen it for yourself." She strutted over to the bars with her nose in the air.

"Yeah? So let me see it now," Jessica said, hugging the side bar.

Dawn scratched her nose, then jumped up to the high bar and began her routine.

Jessica studied Dawn carefully, noticing that her leg was pretty much completely healed. And if her pirouette was as good as she said it was. . . . Suddenly, Jessica felt a knot in her stomach. If Dawn *did* manage to master the pirouette, there was a chance, a *slight* chance that *she'd* bring home the gold at the California Games.

But as Jessica watched Dawn, she saw a more immediate problem. "You're too far over!" she gasped.

Dawn's foot caught on the side bar and she came tumbling down.

Jessica ran over to break Dawn's fall. The force of Dawn's weight knocked them both to the ground.

Jessica brushed the hair out of her face. "You OK?" she asked, shifting a little beneath Dawn's weight.

"Yeah," Dawn muttered as she slowly rolled off Jessica and sat up.

Jessica rubbed her arm where Dawn had fallen against her. "You still think you don't need me?" She cocked her head and grinned at Dawn.

Dawn pursed her lips. "Well, maybe just a little," she admitted with a sniff.

And then she did something that almost made Jessica fall over again. Dawn Maven actually *smiled*.

"OK, people." Coach Arlin clapped her hands together to get everyone's attention. "The California Games are tomorrow. That means today is our last practice."

"Like we don't know that," Lila whispered to Jessica with a giggle. The girls were on the floor stretching out as they listened to Coach Arlin's speech.

"No matter how you all do tomorrow, remember, it's an honor just getting to the California Games," Coach Arlin went on. "You've all worked very hard for this. And I'm proud of each and every one of you."

Jessica glanced up at the clock. Wasn't this a speech that could be saved for the long bus ride to Los Angeles tomorrow? She really wanted to run through her routines.

She fastened her hand grips while her coach finished her speech. "OK," Coach Arlin said finally. "Let's get to work."

Jessica scrambled to her feet and ran for the bars. But Lila beat her to it. She grabbed the low bar possessively and turned to sneer at Jessica.

"Excuse me," Jessica said. "But I'd like to run through my routine."

"Well, I'd like to run through *my* routine!" Lila pouted.

Jessica frowned. "You don't even have your grips on yet. Why don't you just let me run through my routine while you get ready."

"No!" Lila argued. "I was here first so I should get to run through my routine first. Don't think that just because you chose to avoid the bars all those other days you get extra time on them today!"

Jessica glared at Lila. Why shouldn't she get extra time? She was the one who was most likely to bring home the gold medal tomorrow.

"Jessica, why don't you let Lila have a turn on the bars right now and you can work on your beam routine?" Coach Arlin asked reasonably. "Perhaps you can stay a little late tonight and we'll see if we can't do something about tightening some of those moves."

"But I can't stay late," Jessica protested. She'd already missed one of Dawn's practices this week. She wasn't going to miss another. Especially not the last one before the California Games.

But Coach Arlin didn't hear her. She had already moved on to Amy, who was practicing her floor exercise.

"You heard Coach Arlin," Lila said sweetly, nudging Jessica with her hip. "*I* get the first turn on the bars." She bent down and dipped her hands in the chalk.

"Oh, fine!" Jessica unfastened her grips and threw them to the floor.

"Hey!" Lila coughed. "You blew chalk on me!"

"Oh right!" Jessica rolled her eyes. "As if I were anywhere near you!"

"You did!" Lila insisted.

"I did not!" Jessica fumed. "If you want to know what it's like to get chalk on you—" She clapped her hands together right over Lila's beautiful hair.

Lila gasped. She grabbed a handful of chalk and flung it at Jessica.

Jessica coughed. "You're going to get it now," she sputtered as she bent down and grabbed more chalk.

"What's going on over there!" Coach Arlin yelled.

Jessica wiped her face on her shirt in time to see one very angry coach stomping their way. "Uh-oh," she whispered, swallowing hard. She could taste chalk in the back of her mouth.

"With the California Games one day away, I don't know how either of you can spare the time for this foolishness!" she exclaimed, hands on her hips.

Jessica bit her lip and glanced sideways at Lila. There were streaks of white chalk across Lila's face. She shot Jessica a look out of the corner of her eye and then turned away, bored.

"I understand you're feeling a lot of pressure, but that's no excuse for this kind of behavior," Coach Arlin continued. "Now, I want you girls to clean this mess up. And then Lila, you can practice your routine. Jessica, you can stay late and practice yours."

"No, I can't!" Jessica stomped her foot.

This time Ms. Arlin heard. And she did not look pleased.

"I have to leave by four-thirty," Jessica said softly. She couldn't meet her coach's gaze.

"Jessica! I really think we need this one-on-one time," Coach Arlin said firmly.

Jessica felt torn. Part of her felt like she should stay. She should make sure every aspect of her routine was as close to perfect as she could make it. But another part felt like she should be there for Dawn. She already let Dawn down once this week.

But so what? she thought. When did she start caring so much about Dawn Maven?

Some time alone with Coach Arlin could really help your routine, she told herself. *You should concentrate on yourself—not on Dawn.*

But somehow she knew she had to see Dawn one last time before they met in competition. "I'm sorry, Coach Arlin," Jessica said, shaking her head sadly. "I can't stay."

Coach Arlin sighed. "All right, Jessica. Why don't you practice on the beam until Lila has had her turn, and then you can run through your bars routine once before you have to leave."

Jessica nodded and reluctantly headed toward the beam.

"I just can't do it!" Dawn cried. She dropped down from the bars and slammed her fist against the low bar.

"Hey," Jessica said as she walked into the gym. "Take it easy. You don't want to hurt yourself right before a big competition."

"Oh, what do you care?" Dawn narrowed her eyes at Jessica.

Jessica furrowed her brow. "Do you really think I'd be coming over here every day if I didn't care?"

Dawn pulled at her ponytail to tighten it. "You only come because you feel guilty for what you did to me."

Jessica's cheeks burned. Maybe she did feel a little guilty. So what? She still took time out from *her* practice to help Dawn. And she was getting tired of Dawn's attitude.

"I just want to see you get that changeover right so that we're evenly matched at the Games tomorrow," Jessica snapped. "When I beat you, I want it to mean something."

Dawn's face flushed. "You're not going to beat me!"

"I will if you don't get your changeover figured out!"

Dawn frowned as she jumped up to the high bar again.

Jessica watched anxiously as Dawn spun around a few times. Finally, she casted to a handstand. But as usual, she failed to move her hand down far enough for the pirouette. "Argh!" she screamed as her body spun around the bar.

She jumped down. "I hate this!" she yelled as she stomped angrily around the mat.

"I think you need to relax a little," Jessica said uneasily.

"How can I relax?" Dawn screamed. Her eyes blazed with fury. "The California Games are tomorrow! *Tomorrow!* Don't you understand that?"

Jessica gulped and stared wide-eyed at Dawn. She was like a stick of dynamite, ready to go off.

"J-j-just calm down," Jessica said, wringing her hands nervously in front of her. She wasn't sure what would happen if Dawn *really* exploded. "You'll get it if you just calm down!"

"No, I won't." Dawn turned away. She was on the verge of tears. "I don't know what I'm going to do," she moaned, sinking to the floor and hugging her knees to her chest.

Jessica stared at Dawn, trying to breathe steadily. Dawn made it sound like the world would end if her routine wasn't perfect. How could one little problem in her routine push her over the edge like this?

Of course, Jessica wanted her routine to be perfect too. But when she couldn't get something, she didn't lose sleep over it. Maybe that made her a good gymnast instead of a great one. But for once Jessica didn't care about being a *great* gymnast so much. She had enough other things in her life—her friends, the Unicorn Club, parties. She'd sacrifice those things for a couple of weeks right before a competition like the California Games, but she always knew they were there. Even if she wasn't the best gymnast on earth, she still had a lot to be happy about.

Dawn sat on the bench with her head buried in her knees. "Please, just go away," she said as Jessica approached her. There was a catch in her voice.

Jessica sat down beside Dawn and touched her back. It was hard as a rock. "You really shouldn't put yourself under so much pressure," Jessica said softly.

Dawn raised a tear-stained face. "You don't understand. Gymnastics is all I have," she said, looking at Jessica. Then she tilted her head and studied Jessica more closely. "What is all that white stuff all over you?"

Jessica looked down at her shirt and her arms. She grinned sheepishly. "It's chalk. Lila and I both wanted to use the bars at the same time, so we ended up getting into a chalk fight. I didn't want to take the time to clean up. I was afraid I'd miss you."

"A chalk fight!" Dawn snorted as though she couldn't imagine such a thing. "Boy, you and Lila must hate each other a lot."

"*Hate* each other?" Jessica cocked her head and smiled. "Lila and I are best friends."

Dawn's mouth quivered. "I guess I don't know much about having friends," she said, staring at the floor.

Jessica bit her lip. How could anyone not have friends? But she didn't think she should pry. "Maybe we should get back to work," she said softly as she rose to her feet. "Are you ready to get up there and try it again?"

Dawn shrugged. "What's the point? You're the one who's going to win tomorrow. I might as well just drop out."

"Yeah, with an attitude like that, you might as well!" Jessica said, hands on her hips. "What is it with you? If you can't win you don't want to compete?"

Dawn set her jaw. "You don't know anything about me," she spat.

"I know one thing," Jessica said. "You're scared."

Dawn's whole body stiffened. "I am *not!*"

"You are too!" Jessica insisted. "Know how I know?"

"How?" Dawn gave Jessica a cold glance.

Jessica took a deep breath and sat back down. "Because I am too," she admitted in a whisper.

Dawn looked away.

"I never used to be," Jessica continued, flipping her hair over her shoulder. "But ever since you fell, I've been terrified that I'm going to fall too."

"That's ridiculous." Dawn shook her head.

"It's true!" Jessica insisted. "But I forced myself to get back up there. And that's what you have to do too. You have to *force yourself* to pick up that hand and move it when you do your pirouette."

Dawn bit her lip. "I don't know if I can."

"Sure you can," Jessica said, grabbing Dawn's hand and pulling her over to the bars. "I'll do it first. Then you're going to do it!"

Jessica didn't bother putting on her grips. She hopped up to the high bar, swung her legs back and forth a few times, then casted to a handstand. At just the right moment, she picked up her hand and turned it over. *Perfect!*

"See how easy it is?" Jessica asked as she swung back and forth. She changed direction, did a giant swing, and came down in her double flyaway dismount. But she didn't hit the mat quite right. Her right ankle slipped and she fell.

"Ow!" she cried, as a sharp pain cut through her ankle.

Dawn gasped and knelt down in front of Jessica. "Are you OK?" she asked nervously.

Jessica grit her teeth. "Fine," she said, clutching her ankle. She didn't want to put any weight on it just yet, but she also didn't want Dawn fussing over her. "Now you get up there and do what I did!" she commanded as she half-hopped, half-limped off the mat.

Dawn glanced worriedly at Jessica's ankle.

"Do it!" Jessica yelled.

Dawn shrugged as she jumped up to the high bar. She did a couple of practice swings, then casted to the handstand. She held it for a second, turned her hand, and set it down further to the left.

"Yes!" Jessica cried as Dawn's body swung over and she ended up right in the middle of the bar. "You did it!"

Dawn was grinning from ear to ear as she came down. "I can't believe it!" she cried. Her eyes sparkled with pride.

"All it takes is practice," Jessica said, massaging her ankle.

"And overcoming your fear," Dawn added. She hopped back up and did the move again.

"Looks like I'm going to have my work cut out for me competing against you tomorrow." Jessica stood up, careful not to put any weight on her right ankle.

Dawn frowned. "Are you sure you're all right?" she asked.

"I'm fine." Jessica waved her hand dismissively. "I just need to walk it out."

"OK," Dawn said with a sigh. "I guess I'll go get changed."

"Yeah. I better get going too," Jessica said, putting her hands in the pockets of her jacket.

"OK," Dawn replied.

Their eyes met and held. Neither one made a move to leave.

"I uh, guess I'll see you tomorrow," Jessica said finally.

"Yeah." Dawn nodded.

"Good luck," Jessica whispered.

"You too."

*　　　*　　　*

Jessica put her bike in the garage and limped to the house. It had been a long ride home. Every push on the pedal sent a sharp pain shooting through her ankle. *What have I done?* she wondered as she let herself in the back door.

The first thing I need is ice, she told herself, hopping to the freezer. She took the whole tray out, dumped it into a towel, and hopped up to her room.

She closed the door, then hopped to her bed. It felt good to get off that ankle.

She'd managed to squeeze her shoe onto her right foot before she came home, but she hadn't been able to tighten it or tie it. Now, she slipped the shoe off. "Ow!" she cried out in pain as the shoe clattered to the floor.

Next she carefully unrolled her white sock and gently touched the tender spot. She didn't think she'd broken her foot, but she definitely had a good sprain. *And the California Games are tomorrow!*

Jessica couldn't remember how long it took a sprained ankle to heal. But she was pretty sure it was more than twenty-four hours. *What if I can't perform tomorrow?* she thought desperately.

But she had to perform. Somehow she'd manage it, sore ankle or not. This was the *California Games.*

Jessica was touching her wound once more when she heard the front door slam.

"Hello?" Elizabeth called up the stairs. "Jess? Are you home?"

Jessica's stomach knotted. If Elizabeth found out about her ankle, she'd tell their parents, who'd tell Coach Arlin, who'd probably say—

Jessica swallowed hard. No. No one could know about her ankle. Even more important, no one could know where she'd been when she sprained it!

Jessica quickly yanked her covers down and wiggled herself between them. She was just fluffing her pillow behind her back when her bedroom door burst open.

Elizabeth looked puzzled. "What are you doing in bed? We haven't even had dinner yet."

"Oh, yeah, well, we had a killer practice." Jessica yawned dramatically. "I'm beat."

Elizabeth nodded. "But Jess, aren't you *excited* too? You're going to the California Games!" She flopped down on the bed.

Jessica winced. Did Elizabeth have to bounce so hard?

"What?" Elizabeth asked. Worry lines creased her forehead. "Don't you feel good?"

"I'm fine," Jessica replied, shifting her foot away from her sister. "Just tired, like I said before."

"Are you nervous about tomorrow?"

Jessica clucked her tongue. "Why should I be nervous?"

Elizabeth laughed. "Because this is the *California Games!*"

"I'm going to be just fine tomorrow," Jessica insisted. Hopefully saying it out loud would make it come true.

TWELVE

"So tell me, Amy, how does it feel to be on your way to the California Games?" Elizabeth asked in her best reporter voice.

It was Saturday morning and Elizabeth was riding the bus to Los Angeles with the gymnastics team. She wore a white cap with black letters that said Press and carried a spiral notebook in her lap.

Amy squirmed a little on the seat next to Elizabeth. "I can hardly believe it. I'm happy and excited and nervous all at the same time."

Elizabeth furiously scribbled down everything Amy said, then turned to Jessica, who was sitting in the seat across the aisle. She had her foot up on the seat, and she was staring thoughtfully past Elizabeth and Amy, out the window.

"How about you, Jessica?" Elizabeth asked. "Tell

me how it feels to be on the bus heading for the California Games."

Jessica shrugged. "It feels bumpy," she said.

Bumpy? Elizabeth frowned. Jessica had been awfully quiet this morning. Elizabeth expected her twin to be bouncing off the walls with excitement. She'd been dreaming about going to the California Games ever since they were little kids. And now that she was actually going, she didn't have a word to say about it? This wasn't like Jessica at all.

Elizabeth stood up and gave her sister's foot a little nudge. Jessica glanced up at her and slowly brought her foot down so she could sit next to her. "What's the matter, Jess?" Elizabeth asked with concern. "You don't seem very excited."

"I'm just a little nervous," Jessica said, staring at the seat in front of her.

"You? Nervous?" Elizabeth said. "Good thing I've got my notebook so I can record this."

The corners of Jessica's mouth turned up, but she still didn't look at Elizabeth.

"Wow!" Jessica drew in her breath as she gazed around the arena. "This place is huge!"

Bright lights flooded the blue mats, making it hard to see up into the rows and rows of bleachers that circled the entire arena. Jessica knew her parents and brother were up there somewhere, but she had no idea where. In fact, the place was so enormous that Jessica wondered whether they would even be able to see her, wherever they were.

Half a dozen basketball hoops were tucked up

against the ceiling, out of the way, and a huge score-board hung in the middle of the arena.

"Don't you wish we could always compete here?" Lila nudged Jessica, forcing her off balance.

She winced as she came down on her sore foot. "Yeah, that'd be great," she told Lila, stifling a gasp.

"OK, listen up," Coach Arlin said, drawing the team around her in a circle. "I've got the order of events right here." She held up a stack of papers.

I hope I'm on bars first, Jessica thought, crossing her fingers. The bars would put the least amount of stress on her ankle.

"Jessica, you're up first on the bars," Coach Arlin said. "You might want to go and warm up."

Yes! Jessica picked up her bag and tried to walk as normally as possible over to the bars. She could walk with her weight on the side of her foot pretty well. It didn't hurt too much, and she didn't think her limp was noticeable.

I'll just have to take each event as it comes, Jessica told herself as she hobbled past all the girls who were doing stretches on the floor. *Maybe by noon my ankle will be feeling well enough that I can do my other events.*

Her ankle could give out entirely after today and she wouldn't care. But she had to compete in the California Games. She just had to!

Jessica stood with her weight on her left foot and her right toes as she waited for her practice turn at the bars. Finally, the girl on the bars completed her turn with a straddle dismount.

Now it was Jessica's turn. She limped over to the

chalk pan and dipped her hands in it. Then she limped back to the bars and began her warm-up. The straddle and pike positions bothered her ankle a little, but she could handle it. And she had a little trouble standing up on the low bar. But she could put all her weight on her left foot. She'd be OK.

But as she got ready to dismount, it suddenly hit her. How was she going to land a double flyaway on a sprained ankle? She could probably do the two somersaults, but she'd never be able to land on her feet.

There was only one thing to do. She let her body slow down on its own and slowly eased herself down onto the mat. She blinked away the tears that were forming in her eyes. She'd worked so hard on that double flyaway. And now she wasn't going to be able to do it.

"Hello, Jessica," Dawn said solemnly as Jessica bent down to retrieve her towel.

Jessica slowly raised her eyes to Dawn's. "Hi," she replied nervously. Talking to Dawn in Weston's gym was one thing, but somehow talking to her here, before the biggest competition of their lives, felt different.

"How's your ankle?" Dawn asked timidly.

"Oh, it's fine." Jessica waved her hand like it didn't matter. "I, uh, think I'm ready to compete against you."

"I think I'm ready to compete against you too," Dawn said.

"Good." Jessica nodded. She didn't know what else to say.

"Well, I'll see you," Dawn said, backing away slowly.

"Yeah." Jessica waved. "See ya."

Jessica's heart leaped when the announcer called her to the bars. *This is it!*

"Come on, Jessica!" Lila slapped her on the back. "We're counting on you to put us on the board."

Jessica nodded. So far, Team Sweet Valley wasn't doing so great. Amy had scored a 9.2 on the floor exercise, but a girl from El Carro had scored a 9.3 and Dawn had scored a 9.4. It was up to Jessica to put Team Sweet Valley on the scoreboard.

Jessica tried to make her walk over to the mat look as normal as possible. She forced herself to ignore the pain in her ankle. People were definitely watching her now.

Her heart was pounding as she put on her grips and chalked them up. She'd never felt so nervous before a competition. But then again, she'd never competed at the California Games before either.

As she took her place on the mat, she could feel sweat dotting her palms. She took a deep breath.

"You can do it, Jessica!" she heard Donald Zwerdling call out behind her.

Jessica signaled to the judges and began her routine. She felt light as a bird as she soared up and over the bars. *I'm not going to fall,* she told herself. *I'm not going to fall.*

And she didn't. She whipped through one move after another. *This might be my best performance yet,* she thought as she went into her handstand and pirouette.

All that was left now was the giant swing and her dismount. Everything had gone so well up until now that she was tempted to try the double flyaway dismount. But she knew there was no way she'd land it on a sprained ankle.

All that work down the drain, Jessica thought miserably as tears blurred her vision.

She attempted a straight layaway dismount, but she couldn't even land that. Her sore ankle gave out and she fell to her knees.

"Jessica! You're limping! Are you hurt?" Coach Arlin cried as she rushed to Jessica's side. Lila was right behind her.

"Two questions, Jessica." Lila's jaw was set firmly. "Why didn't you do the double flyaway and how could you possibly not land a simple layaway?"

"Lila!" Coach Arlin said with an annoyed glance over her shoulder. "This is neither the time nor the place. Jessica, did you just land funny or are you really hurt?" Worry showed in her blue eyes.

"I'm fine, Coach Arlin," Jessica lied as she sank down on the bench. "Everything was just going so well that I choked on the dismount. I'm really sorry."

"It's OK!" Coach Arlin squeezed her shoulders. "You still did a very good job."

Jessica chewed her lip as she waited for her score. She needed a 9.3 to beat the girl from Big Mesa. *Please, oh please!* she prayed silently. Even though she blew her dismount, the rest of her routine was practically flawless.

"9.4!" the head judge announced. "9.4!"

"Yay! Hooray!" Everyone on the Sweet Valley bench jumped up and screamed.

Jessica was in the lead for now. But Dawn hadn't competed yet.

Jessica couldn't take her eyes off Dawn. Her routine was going really well. But she hadn't come to her pirouette yet.

Would she get that hand change or wouldn't she? Jessica wondered nervously. She couldn't help smiling. It was strange, but she was almost more nervous for Dawn than she'd been for herself.

Jessica held her breath as Dawn went up into her handstand. *Come on. Pick your hand up and move it down the bar.*

And Dawn did! Her changeover was perfect. She ended up right in the middle of the bar.

"All right!" Jessica shouted, pumping her fist in the air.

Lila nudged Jessica. "What's so big about a few dance steps?" she asked.

"Huh?" Jessica asked.

Lila nodded toward Mary Wallace, who was performing her floor exercise. "Her big move is coming up. Watch."

Jessica bit her lip. Lila thought Jessica had been cheering for Mary. *I guess I should be paying more attention to my own teammate,* Jessica thought. But after a brief glance at Mary's series of flight moves, Jessica turned back to Dawn, who was just finishing up. She came barreling through the bars with her straddle leg dismount and landed it right on.

The crowd in the stands cheered. Jessica couldn't see them, but she could hear them. And Dawn's teammates jumped up and down, waving their blue flags, shouting, "Yay, Dawn!"

Jessica sprang up and moved as fast as she could on a sore ankle. "Dawn!" she yelled, waving her arms. She hopped on one foot all the way to the bars, where she threw her arms around Dawn. "You did it!" she cried.

"I know," Dawn said, hugging Jessica back.

"Jessica!" a voice yelled.

Jessica's heart stopped. It was Coach Arlin. And behind her stood Lila, Mary, and Amy. *They all think I'm a traitor,* Jessica thought as her heart leaped into her throat. How could she possibly explain what she was doing over here hugging Dawn Maven, her biggest rival?

But nobody was asking for any explanations. They were all staring at her ankle.

THIRTEEN

Dawn Maven felt a stab of jealousy as she watched a whole entourage of people lead Jessica back to her bench. *When I hurt my ankle, my coach came out to help me, but none of my teammates did,* Dawn thought.

Dawn's score flashed on the large board in the middle of the gym. 9.6! She beat Jessica, which put Weston in the lead.

"All right!" Wendy Potter jumped up and cheered.

"Way to go, Dawn!" Melissa Rice clapped.

Dawn slapped a high five with Kelly Smith, but her heart wasn't in it. These girls weren't her friends, not the way Jessica's teammates were *her* friends. They ran on ahead without her, whispering and giggling excitedly among themselves. They didn't even ask her to join them.

But what did she expect? She wasn't one of them.

They did gymnastics for the season. Dawn did it year-round. She practiced five days a week for four hours each day. Her dream was to make it to the Olympics. And she knew the only way that would happen is if she made gymnastics her life.

Dawn glanced across the gym at Jessica, who was sitting on the bench with her leg propped up. She was surrounded by teammates and friends, and they were all talking and laughing.

Jessica was so stupid, Dawn thought. *Why did she have to help me with my changeover anyway?* If she hadn't, *she* might have won today.

Dawn remembered how Jessica had said this competition was really between the two of them, and that if they couldn't compete fair and square, the victory wouldn't mean anything. Dawn understood now what Jessica had meant. For the first time in her life, her victory felt hollow.

There was a doctor wrapping Jessica's ankle now. Dawn wanted to go over and talk to Jessica, but she didn't know what to say. And now that the scores had been posted, Jessica probably wouldn't speak to her anyway.

Jessica sat with her leg propped up and a towel of ice wrapped around it. The awards ceremony was about to begin.

Coach Arlin had brought her a pillow, Elizabeth had brought her a Coke, and Donald Zwerdling had brought her a candy bar. This was the life!

"A silver medal on the bars!" Coach Arlin shook her head. "I'm amazed you were able to perform so well with an ankle that was giving you so much trouble." Jessica had admitted her ankle had actually been bothering her since yesterday. That was why she had avoided the double flyaway.

Jessica tossed her hair over her shoulder. "What can I say? I'm just good."

"And modest too," Donald added. He and Elizabeth laughed.

"Well, if Dawn hadn't figured out that changeover, you probably would have taken the gold in the bars competition," Coach Arlin told her.

Jessica smiled faintly. She glanced over at Dawn, who was surrounded by reporters. *That could have been me,* she thought with a tinge of jealousy. Then she giggled to herself. *That could have been me if it* weren't *for me.* In a way, after all the help she'd given Dawn, she felt like Dawn's gold medal was half hers. Half of a gold medal, plus a silver medal from the California Games was nothing to complain about. Especially when you did it on a sprained ankle.

Andy Pride, a sports commentator for ABC was announcing the winners from the podium at the center of the arena. "And now, the uneven parallel bars competition," Andy said.

Jessica sat up a little straighter.

"Are you going to be able to walk out to the podium by yourself?" Elizabeth asked with a worried frown.

"Of course!" Jessica replied with a smile. "I walked out to the bars and did my routine by myself. So I can certainly go claim my medal by myself!" She undid the towel that was wrapped around her leg.

"In third place, taking home the bronze medal for Big Mesa Middle School, Alena Walker!" Andy announced.

Polite applause sounded from all corners of the arena as a girl with a long auburn ponytail and red-and-white leotard went to stand on the third-place step.

"And in second place," Andy continued, "taking home the silver medal for Sweet Valley Middle School, Jessica Wakefield!"

Jessica slapped hands with her sister and all the members of her team. Then she limped across the gym to take her place on the second step of the podium. "Hooray, Jessica!" the audience whistled and cheered. Jessica turned around on her step and waved as several flashbulbs went off.

The head judge put a silver medal around Jessica's neck and handed her a bouquet of roses. Jessica breathed in the smell of the flowers. This was so great!

"And in first place, bringing home the gold medal for Weston Middle School, Dawn Maven!"

The cheers were louder for Dawn than they'd been for Jessica. And there were even more flashbulbs. *But when they clap for her, they're also clapping for me,* Jessica reminded herself. *If it wasn't for me Dawn never would've figured out that changeover.*

Dawn smiled shyly at Jessica as she stepped up to the highest spot on the podium. As the head judge placed the gold medal around Dawn's neck and presented her with a bouquet of roses, Dawn grabbed

Jessica's hand. "I couldn't have done it without you," she whispered.

Jessica squeezed Dawn's hand. "Don't you forget it," she whispered back.

Dawn raised an eyebrow and Jessica smiled.

"And we have one more award to give out this afternoon," Andy Pride went on. "The award for Most Promising Gymnast. This award is given to the gymnast who has the highest overall score on all four apparatuses. The winner will receive a gym bag courtesy of Maurice, a gift certificate from Sports Are Us for gymnastics apparel, two weeks at the nearest intercollegiate gymnastics camp, and ten thousand dollars in college scholarship money."

Jessica looked at Dawn, who was biting her lip. Besides the gold medal she took on the bars, she also took a gold on the balance beam and a bronze on the floor exercise. She had a real shot at that award.

"This year's Most Promising Gymnast Award goes to . . . Dawn Maven!"

Dawn clasped her hands to her cheeks as the audience stomped and cheered.

Jessica nudged Dawn. "Go get your prize," she said.

Dawn stood at the podium, clearing her throat. Gradually, the applause died away. "Uh, I want to say thank you to my coach, Mr. Wykoff, to my team, and to my parents for all their encouragement," she said into the microphone. "But there's one other person I really need to thank. And that's my opponent and friend, Jessica Wakefield."

Dawn turned to Jessica, and with the plaque and

the two bouquets held tight in the crook of her arm, she started clapping. Soon the audience joined in.

Jessica stared at Dawn in astonishment. Then she glanced around the arena. Everyone on the floor was applauding her too.

A huge smile spread across her face. Dawn may have taken first place, but Jessica was a real star too. She knew it, Dawn knew it, and now *everyone* knew it.

Jessica was carefully slipping her shoe on over her swollen foot when Dawn approached her. Her hair hung loose around her shoulders and she carried her ratty gym bag. "Uh, we're just getting ready to leave," she said.

"Yeah, so are we," Jessica told her.

Dawn licked her lips. "Um—I just want to say I'm sorry," she said, staring at her feet. "You know. For rubbing oil on the bars that day."

Jessica looked at Dawn in surprise. She could only imagine how hard it was for Dawn to say those words.

"We only had two more chances to qualify for the California Games," Dawn continued in a rush. "And I was afraid you were going to beat me every time. I wanted to go to the California Games more than anything else in the whole world! Can you, uh, ever forgive me?" she stammered. There were tears in her eyes.

"I can forgive you," Jessica said as she pulled Dawn into a hug. "Can you forgive me for putting sugar in your chalk?" she whispered in Dawn's ear.

Dawn pulled away. She looked quizzically at Jessica. "Is that what you did? You put sugar in the chalk?"

Jessica nodded sheepishly and Dawn burst out laughing.

"I can forgive you," Dawn said, dabbing at the corners of her eyes. Then she cleared her throat. "Will I ever see you again?" she asked anxiously.

"Of course," Jessica replied. "Our schools play each other all the time. I'll see you next season. And I'll beat the pants off you then!" She slugged Dawn in the arm.

Dawn smiled. "We'll see about that."

Created by FRANCINE PASCAL

Follow the adventures of Jessica and Elizabeth and all their friends at Sweet Valley as twelve-year-olds. A super series with one new title every month.

Ask your bookseller for any titles you may have missed. the Sweet Valey Twins series is published by Bantam books.

Created by FRANCINE PASCAL

We hope you enjoyed reading this book. If you would like to receive further information about available titles in the Bantam series, just write to the address below, with your name and address:

KIM PRIOR
Bantam Books
61–63 Uxbridge Road
London W5 5SA

If you live in Australia or New Zealand and would like more information about the series, please write to:

SALLY PORTER
Transworld Publishers (Australia) Pty Ltd
15–25 Helles Avenue
Moorebank
NSW 2170
AUSTRALIA

KIRI MARTIN
Transworld Publishers (NZ) Ltd
3 William Pickering Drive
Albany
Auckland
NEW ZEALAND

All Transworld titles are available by post from:-
Bookservice by Post
PO Box 29
Douglas
Isle of Man
IM991BQ

Credit Cards accepted. Please telephone 01624 675137
or fax 01624 670923

Please allow £0.75 per book for post and packing UK.
Overseas customers allow £1.00 per book for post and packing.